ENTANGLE

DIVYA DISM

ENTANGLE

This masterpiece is brought to you by none other than me, DIVYA DISM. I owe myself a huge thanks for the sleepless nights, the endless rewrites, and the audacity to believe in my brilliance. To the person who never gave up—you did it.

DIVYA DISM

Contents

1

Dana had grown up surrounded by luxury—mansions, vacations, designer clothes. It was a life most people would dream of. But for Dana, there was always something missing: friends her own age. Being homeschooled all her life had made her shy, nervous, and unsure of how to act around other people. Today was different, though. Today, for the first time, she was stepping into a real college. Her heart thudded in her chest as she walked across the campus, surrounded by the chatter and energy of students rushing to class.

The college was as lively as she'd imagined, maybe even more so. People filled the hallways, laughing, sharing inside jokes, and calling out to each other. Dana swallowed her nerves and scanned the room, quickly noticing two people who seemed to be the center of everyone's attention.

Catherine was the queen of the school. She was the girl everyone wanted to be friends with, and the one all the guys tried to impress. Then there was Ethan, the mysterious and insanely cool guy. He was so handsome that girls couldn't stop staring, but he always seemed a little distant, like he didn't care much about anything.

Rumor had it that Catherine and Ethan were secretly dating because they were always together, laughing and whispering. But whenever anyone asked, they just rolled their eyes and laughed it off.

Dana walked into her first class, her hands clammy and her face flushed. She chose a seat in the back corner, hoping to blend in. She glanced up just as Catherine's eyes met hers. Dana looked down immediately, pretending to be busy with her notebook, but it was too late.

"Hey! You're new, right?" Catherine's voice was friendly and warm. She slid into the seat next to Dana without waiting for an answer. "Mind if I sit here?"

Dana's cheeks turned pink. "Um, sure. That's okay."

Catherine grinned, flipping her hair over her shoulder. "I'm Catherine. This is, like, the best class, mostly because our professor tells the worst jokes. You'll love it."

Dana nodded and felt a slight smile spread across her face, even though she hadn't expected it.. By the end of class, Catherine had introduced Dana to nearly everyone in their row, sprinkling her stories with quick, funny comments that made everyone laugh. For the first time in forever, Dana felt her nerves start to loosen.

Lunch was even better. Dana found herself at a table with Catherine and, to her surprise, Ethan. He was quieter than she expected but had a way of making dry comments that cracked her up. "So, what do you think of the campus so far?" Ethan asked, looking at her with an expression that was impossible to read.

"It's... big," Dana managed, her heart fluttering at the attention.

Catherine laughed, "Took me a year to find the best shortcuts. Stick with us, and we'll show you all the secret spots."

The day ended with Dana feeling a little giddy. She hadn't expected to find friends so soon, and definitely not ones like Catherine and Ethan. That night, in the privacy of her luxurious room, Dana scribbled in her diary. "Today was awesome! I made two new friends, Catherine and Ethan. Ethan... well, he's just really cool." She paused, biting her lip, wanting to write more about Ethan, but feeling too shy.

Over the next few weeks, Dana, Catherine, and Ethan became a trio. They ate lunch together, studied in the library until closing time, and shared jokes that made Dana's cheeks hurt from laughing. But something kept gnawing at her. Every time Catherine leaned over to whisper something to Ethan or when they burst out laughing at an inside joke, Dana felt a knot in her stomach.

One afternoon, after a long study session, Dana blurted out, "Hey, what if we did something fun this weekend? Like a picnic by the lake?"

Catherine's eyes lit up. "That's a fantastic idea! We can pack sandwiches and snacks, maybe even bring cards to play or something fun like that."

"Yeah, why not?" Ethan said, giving Dana a small smile that made her heart flip.

The day of the picnic was perfect. The sun was warm, and the breeze carried the smell of wildflowers. They spread out a blanket under a big oak tree, laughing as they passed around sandwiches and chips. Ethan leaned back on his elbows, eyes half-closed as he listened to Catherine's stories, but he'd look at Dana every now and then, giving her a soft smile that felt like a secret.

"I had so much fun today," Dana said as they packed up their things to leave.

"Me too," Ethan said, his eyes meeting hers.

"Definitely! We need to do this again soon," Catherine chimed in, throwing her arm around Dana's shoulders.

Dana forced a smile, but her heart sank. It wasn't that she didn't like Catherine—she did. But she wished, just for once, that it could be her and Ethan alone.

That night, Dana poured her thoughts onto the page. *Today was perfect. But I wish I could have had more time with Ethan. Catherine is always there, and it's getting harder not to feel jealous.* She sighed and shut her diary, staring at the ceiling.

Over the next few days, the feeling grew stronger. Dana didn't want to resent Catherine—she was kind, funny, and had welcomed her with open arms. But as Dana found herself watching Ethan from across the table or catching moments between him and Catherine, she knew something had to change. She just hadn't realized how complicated things would get when she finally decided to act.

2

The clock struck midnight, and Dana's parents quietly crept into her room, their faces glowing with excitement. "Happy Birthday, Dana!" they sang, their voices full of warmth and love.

Dana opened her eyes, groggy at first, but quickly woke up to see her room transformed. Streamers hung from the ceiling, balloons floated in the air, and a huge banner with *"Happy Birthday, Dana!"* was taped to the wall. Her heart skipped a beat. It was like stepping into a dream.

"Make a wish, sweetheart," her dad said, holding a cake with flickering candles.

Closing her eyes, Dana thought of Ethan, the boy who had unknowingly stolen her heart. *"I wish Ethan and I could be together,"* she whispered to herself before blowing out the candles in one go.

Her dad smiled and handed her a small, shiny key. "Here's your present, Dana."

Dana stared at the key in confusion. "What's this for?"

"It's the key to your very own park," her dad announced with pride, showing her a photo of a lush green space filled with swings, slides, and climbing walls.

"Wait... WHAT?" Dana gasped.

"Yup! It's all yours. Just promise to let other kids enjoy it too," he teased with a wink.

Before Dana could recover from the shock, her dad pulled out another surprise. "There's more. Remember that secret bunker you always wanted inside the pool?" He held up a photo of a sleek, futuristic space with cozy lounges, a mini-game zone, and even some gadgets she'd sketched in her childhood drawings.

Dana was speechless. Her parents had gone above and beyond her wildest dreams. "I... I can't believe it!" she squealed, throwing her arms around them. Her heart felt full, and her mind raced with plans for the day ahead.

Swimming had always been her way to find peace, and having a special place in the pool where she could escape and relax was a dream come true. That night, she drifted off to sleep with a big smile, excited for what was to come.

The next morning, Dana walked into college, turning heads in a dress that made her look effortlessly stunning. She spotted Ethan almost immediately.

"Wow, Dana, you look amazing!" Ethan blurted out before he could stop himself.

Dana's heart soared. For a moment, it was just the two of them, and she forgot all about Catherine, who was standing nearby with a polite smile.

Catherine handed Dana a box of pastries. "Happy birthday, Dana."

"Thank you, Catherine," Dana said sweetly, but her mind was already racing. She had plans—big plans.

As Catherine excused herself to head to the restroom, Dana seized the moment. She leaned in toward Ethan and handed him a small note. "There's a party at my park tonight. You should come," she whispered, her voice filled with hope.

Ethan smiled, tucking the note into his pocket. Dana couldn't help but feel a flicker of confidence. Maybe tonight would be the start of something special.

Dana told herself, "Maybe Catherine has plans for the evening. Besides, she probably has evening classes." She was determined to get closer to Ethan.

That evening, the park was alive with laughter, music, and the mouthwatering aroma of freshly grilled food. Dana looked radiant as she welcomed her guests, her eyes constantly scanning the crowd for Ethan.

Finally, she saw him walking toward the park—but her heart sank when she noticed Catherine by his side. She clung to Ethan's arm, her smile radiant, as if she knew exactly what she was doing.

Dana shook off the disappointment. She wasn't going to let this ruin her night. Taking the mic, she announced a game. "Alright, everyone! Here's the deal: Every guy picks a girl and carries her to the finish line. The winner gets a thousand bucks!"

The crowd erupted in cheers, and Dana silently hoped Ethan would choose her. But before she could even move, Catherine's eyes lit up at the mention of the prize, Catherine grabbed Ethan's hand. "Come on, Ethan!" she said, dragging him to the starting line.

Dana watched as Ethan lifted Catherine into his arms. They laughed together as they raced to the finish line, leaving Dana standing frozen, her excitement fading with every step they took.

When the game ended and Ethan and Catherine were declared the winners, Dana forced a smile, clapping along with the crowd. But inside, her heart ached.

Later, she pulled Catherine aside. "Hey, are you and Ethan... dating?" Dana asked, trying to sound casual, though her voice betrayed her frustration.

Catherine's lips curled into a sly smile. "Well, Ethan and I are..." she began, but before she could finish, her phone buzzed. She glanced at the screen and her expression changed.

"Oh shoot, it's my teacher!" Catherine said hurriedly. "I totally forgot about evening classes!" She grabbed her bag and dashed off, leaving Dana with more questions than answers.

As the party wound down, Dana found herself sitting on a swing, gently rocking back and forth. Ethan sat on the swing beside her, the two of them wrapped in silence.

This was her chance.

"Ethan," she said softly, her voice barely above a whisper. "I love you."

Ethan froze, then let out an awkward laugh. "You know, actually I am..." he began, but then stopped himself. He looked at her for a moment, as if deciding something, then shook his head. "Never mind. I'm just really tired. See you tomorrow at college." Dana raised an eyebrow, a small smile tugging at her lips. "Ethan, it's Sunday tomorrow," she reminded him. He blinked, then let out a short laugh. "Oh, right. Well, see you on Monday then,"

He stood up and walked away, leaving Dana alone under the stars, her heart heavier than ever.

She stared at the empty swing beside her, the echoes of Ethan's laughter still ringing in her ears. But despite the pain, Dana wasn't ready to give up. Not yet. She was determined to uncover the truth—about Catherine, about Ethan, and about where she truly stood in his life. Dana thought to herself, Ethan didn't say anything when I told him I love him... maybe he just needs some time. He didn't exactly reject me, so there's still a chance, she comforted herself with a small smile.

It was Sunday, and Catherine was cleaning her room. The room had once belonged to her mom, but now her mom was no longer in this world. Catherine had never known her mom well since she had passed away when Catherine was just a baby. As she was tidying up, her eyes caught a small, old box tucked away in a drawer. Curiosity got the best of her, and she opened it to find a vintage ring inside. She immediately thought it might have been her mother's.

Without thinking too much, Catherine slipped the ring onto her finger, and just as she did, her phone rang. It was Dana.

"Hey, Catherine! Meet me at the park later today, okay? I need to talk to you," Dana's voice came through the phone.

Catherine stared at the ring on her finger for a moment longer, feeling a strange sense of calm wash over her, then nodded to herself. "Sure, I'll be there," she replied, wondering what Dana wanted to talk about.

When Catherine finally showed up, Dana stood up and took a deep breath. "Catherine, I'm being serious. I really want to know—are you and Ethan dating?" she asked, her voice steady but anxious.

Catherine, trying to hold back her laughter, walked dramatically to the pool. She turned back to Dana with a mischievous glint in her eye. "Actually, Ethan and I are dating," she said with a sly smile, enjoying Dana's reaction. In reality, Catherine was just joking and wanted to see how Dana would react.

But Dana, unable to handle the shock, marched up to Catherine and, in a moment of impulsive frustration, pushed her into the pool. What Dana didn't know was that Catherine was hydrophobic and didn't know how to swim.

Dana stood frozen, watching Catherine struggle in the water. After two minutes of Catherine not surfacing, Dana's panic kicked in. Without thinking, she jumped into the pool and searched for Catherine. Ten minutes later, she emerged alone, her heart pounding but a smile on her face.

Dana walked home in her wet clothes, and her mom asked, "Why are you soaking wet?"

Dana shrugged, trying to sound casual. "I really wanted to swim and didn't have a swimsuit, so I just went for it. Sorry, Mom." She went to her room, chuckling to herself. "Finally, I feel good! I'm so excited for tomorrow!" She wrote in her diary, her trusted friend, and went to bed with a contented smile.

The next morning, Dana got ready for college, feeling unusually cheerful. When she arrived, she saw Ethan waiting for Catherine, who was late. Ethan tried calling her, but there was no answer. "Maybe she's already at college," he thought and headed to class.

In class, Dana spotted Ethan and waved at him with a bright smile. "Hi, Ethan!"

Ethan looked surprised. "Hey, Dana. Have you seen Catherine?"

"No, I haven't," Dana replied, trying to sound nonchalant. "She must be tired from studying and going to tuitions. Maybe she needs some rest."

Ethan frowned. "It's unlike her not to let me know if she's going to be late. I'll check on her after college."

During class, Dana made an effort to sit closer to Ethan, making cute faces and laughing, thrilled to be spending time alone with him. After the class, she asked, "Hey, how about we grab something tasty?"

Ethan hesitated. "I'd love to, but I need to check on Catherine first."

Dana quickly said, "Come on, Ethan. She's grown up and can handle herself. She needs some personal space."

Ethan considered this and then said, "Okay, how about we have lunch first, and then we'll visit Catherine's place together? I want to see if you really care about her."

Dana agreed, feeling a flutter of excitement as she sat on Ethan's bike. She shyly held onto his shoulders as they rode. They enjoyed a delicious meal before heading to Catherine's apartment.

When they arrived, Ethan rang the doorbell, but there was no response. He called Catherine's phone, but it went straight to voicemail. "I know the password," he said, leading Dana inside.

Dana felt a mix of worry and excitement, knowing what had happened but enjoying the time alone with Ethan. Inside, Ethan called out for Catherine, but there was no reply.

Dana noticed some family photos on the wall and asked, "Ethan, who are these people?"

Ethan looked at the pictures and said, "That's my family."

Dana was confused. "Why is your family photo in Catherine's room?"

Ethan explained, "This is my mom and dad, and this is my twin sister, Catherine. And this is me, her twin brother, born 369 seconds later."

Dana's eyes widened in shock. "Wait, what? You and Catherine are twins?"

Ethan nodded. "Yes. We're just siblings who behave like besties. We used to fight a lot, but once we started behaving like best friends, everything got better. Catherine's always been there for me."

Dana's face fell. "So, you and Catherine aren't dating?"

Ethan laughed. "No, Catherine must have been joking with you. We are just siblings who behave like besties."

Dana's heart sank. "Then why don't you love me?"

Ethan sighed. "It's not that. I'm really into you as a friend, but I'm actually gay."

Dana was overwhelmed. She had never expected this and felt her world spinning. Tears filled her eyes, and she ran out, crying.

Dana burst through the door, pale and panicked. "Mom! Dad!" she cried, her voice shaking. "I don't know what to do. I'm so sorry."

"I... I killed someone," Dana whispered. "Catherine... I pushed her into the pool. She didn't know how to swim. I thought she did, but she didn't come up. I went in, and she was unconscious. I thought she was dead, so I took her to the bunker under the pool and left her there."

Her parents froze. Her dad's voice was cold. "Is she dead?"

Dana nodded, tears streaming. "I didn't know what else to do."

Her dad's expression hardened. "We're not going to the police. We protect our own."

"Pack your things," he ordered. "We leave tonight."

Dana's guilt was overwhelming, but she did as he said. And just like that, they left Silverbay, disappearing into the night.

Ethan sat alone in his room, his eyes glued to his phone. He had called Catherine over and over, but there was no answer. She hadn't been at college, and now she was nowhere to be found. His chest tightened, the worry building up as he thought of every possible worst-case scenario. Something wasn't right.

He grabbed his phone again and called his dad. His voice wavered when Darwen picked up.

"Dad, is Catherine at your place?" Ethan asked, trying to keep his voice calm.

Darwen paused, sounding confused. "What do you mean? Shouldn't she be with you?"

"No... she isn't anywhere," Ethan said quickly, his words tumbling out. "She didn't show up at college today. I'm freaking out, Dad. I don't know where she is."

There was silence on the other end, then Darwen's voice came back, steady but with a hint of worry. "Don't worry, I'll be there. I'm just a few hours away from Silverbay."

Ethan let out a shaky breath. "Okay. Just... hurry."

A few hours later, Darwen was in his car, heading toward Silverbay. His mind was racing, but there was a familiar heaviness sitting on his chest. As he drove, his eyes flicked to the rearview mirror. Hanging from it was a scarf. A scarf that belonged to Seraphina, the woman he thought he'd spend his whole life with. The memory of her hit him like a punch to the gut. She was gone. Gone forever. And he could still feel the weight of that loss pressing on him. His thoughts drifted back to the past, back to the first day of his pre-university days.

THE PAST (20 YEARS AGO)

It was the first day of pre-university. Darwen was confident, outgoing, and friendly. People loved being around him, and he thrived in the spotlight. He was the guy everyone wanted to be friends with.

The professor walked in, and students began scrambling for seats. A girl walked into the room, drawing attention with her easy smile and graceful confidence. She scanned the room, her eyes falling on the empty seat next to a guy.

She approached him with a soft smile. "Hey, is anyone sitting here?"

He froze, his throat suddenly dry. His heart thudded in his chest. "U-uh, no," he stammered, barely audible.

"Cool," she said, sliding into the chair. "I'm Seraphina, but you can call me Sera."

He nodded awkwardly, keeping his gaze fixed on his notebook. "Okay..." he muttered.

She tilted her head, studying him for a moment before asking, "And what about you? What's your name?"

"Morwen," he said quickly, his voice barely above a whisper.

"Well, Morwen, nice to meet you." Her tone was light, cheerful, as though they'd known each other forever. She started talking, sharing bits about herself, her hometown, and how she was excited yet nervous about this new chapter in her life.

Morwen didn't say much, only nodding occasionally, his eyes never quite meeting hers. It wasn't that he wasn't listening—he was. In fact, he was hanging onto every word, but he didn't know how to respond.

When the class ended, Sera packed her things and turned to him. "See you tomorrow, Morwen," she said with a smile.

Morwen managed a small nod, watching as she walked away.

Sera was walking down the street, her bag slung over her shoulder. The evening air was crisp, and she was humming a tune under her breath. Ahead, she spotted Darwen walking in the same direction.

"Hey!" she called out, quickening her pace to catch up to him.

Darwen turned, startled. He hadn't noticed her behind him. "Oh, hey," he said, his surprise evident.

"You're in my class, right?" she asked, falling into step beside him.

"Uh, yeah," Darwen replied, his usual confidence faltering slightly under her gaze.

"I'm Sera. And you are...?" she prompted.

"Darwen," he said. "So, do you live around here?"

"Yeah, I live in a studio apartment a few blocks from here," he replied. "What about you?"

"Same," she said, her voice warm. "My mom lives in Cloverfield, but since the education is better here in Silverbay, I moved here."

Darwen nodded, intrigued. "That's pretty independent of you. What about friends? Made any yet?"

"Well, I talked to Morwen today," she said, her tone thoughtful. "He's... quiet. I feel like I did all the talking."

Darwen chuckled. "That sounds like Morwen. He's my twin brother, actually."

"Twin?!" Sera's eyes widened in surprise. "You two are nothing alike!"

"Yeah, we're pretty different," Darwen admitted. "He's more... reserved. We don't talk much. I've kind of learned to leave him be."

Sera nodded, processing the information. "Well, he seems sweet. Just shy, I guess."

They walked in silence for a moment before Darwen glanced at her. "So... do you believe in love?"

She stopped, tilting her head at the unexpected question. "Yeah, of course. I mean, I love my mom more than anything. Without love, what's the point of living?"

Darwen felt a pang in his chest at her words, her sincerity pulling at something deep inside him. "I guess I do too," he said after a moment. "But I don't really say it. I'm more of a 'show it, don't say it' kind of person."

Sera smiled at him, a soft, understanding smile that seemed to light up the dim street. "That's fair. Sometimes actions speak louder than words, anyway."

Darwen found himself smiling back, his usual confidence returning as he looked into her eyes. He didn't know it then, but this moment, this chance encounter, would change everything.

And somewhere behind the window of his studio apartment, Morwen watched them walk together, his heart heavier than he could understand.

5

Every day was a beautiful day for Darwen and Seraphina.

Their bond grew deeper with each passing moment, and their shared walks from college to their studio apartments became their sanctuary. These quiet walks, filled with laughter, lighthearted teasing, and deep conversations, were where their connection truly blossomed. They eagerly awaited the end of each class, knowing that their time together was the highlight of their day.

One day, as exams approached, Darwen invited Seraphina to his studio apartment to study.The air was calm but charged, a quiet tension lingering as they poured over their books. Seraphina sat cross-legged on the floor, scribbling notes, while Darwen leaned over the table, flipping through pages of a thick textbook.

"This part here is so confusing," she muttered, biting her lip.

Darwen looked up with a soft smile. "Don't worry. We'll figure it out together."

His calm confidence eased her worries, but Seraphina found herself distracted. She watched him as he focused, his brows furrowed and his hair slightly tousled. Her heart raced, and she couldn't ignore the pull any longer. In a sudden rush of emotion, she leaned forward, cupped his face with her hands, and kissed him gently.

Darwen froze, his eyes wide in surprise. Seraphina pulled back, her cheeks flushed a deep red. She couldn't look at him as she quickly stammered, "You said you weren't the type to say you loved someone with words... that you'd show it instead. So, I just thought... I'd do it too. Instead of saying it." She exhaled, her words tumbling out in one nervous breath.

Darwen's silence stretched for a moment. Then, to her surprise, he broke into a smile, his cheeks tinged pink. "You started it," he murmured, his voice low and warm, "so now it's my turn to show you."

Without hesitation, he wrapped his arms around her, lifting her effortlessly. Seraphina let out a soft gasp as he carried her to his bed, his eyes never leaving hers. He kissed her deeply, pouring all his unspoken feelings into that moment. As their emotions collided, everything else seemed to fade away.

And the rest, as they say, was history.

They spent their pre-university days like this—in secret, stealing moments of love and joy. No one really knew about them, not even Darwen's twin brother, Morwen.

Meanwhile, Morwen, Darwen's twin brother, was quietly struggling with his own feelings. For months, he had harbored a growing crush on Seraphina. Her laugh, her smile, the way she talks—everything about her captivated him. But Morwen was too shy, too afraid to confess his feelings.

Unbeknownst to him, his twin brother and Seraphina were already in a relationship, sharing the very moments Morwen longed for.

As the final days of pre-university life approached, Morwen made a decision.

He would go abroad to study medicine. "I'll build myself up," he told himself, staring at his packed suitcase. "When I come back, I'll finally ask her out." He smiled softly at the thought of winning Seraphina's heart. He clutched a small photo of Seraphina that he'd secretly taken during a campus event. The hope in his heart outweighed the pain of leaving.

But little did he know, the love he dreamed of, the love he was working so hard to win, was already someone else's reality. His own twin brother was living the life he longed for, sharing the moments he yearned to create.

When the results came out, the transition to university life began. Darwen and Seraphina, inseparable as ever, enrolled in the same university, excited to face this new chapter together. Their love had only grown stronger, and they promised to keep their relationship private for now, savoring the intimacy of their secret.

Morwen, on the other hand, boarded a plane to his new life abroad. As he sat by the window, gazing at the clouds, his heart was filled with hope and determination. "This is just the beginning," he thought. "When I come back, everything will be different." He and Darwen had never gotten along, and they rarely spoke.

Darwen had no idea Morwen was leaving. Morwen had always felt overshadowed by Darwen—his outgoing, charming twin who took up all the attention. No one noticed Morwen when Darwen was around. So, he pulled away, distancing himself more and more, until they barely spoke at all.

But fate had other plans. The truth he was unaware of loomed in the background, waiting to unravel. The love he had hoped for was already spoken for, entwined in a story he couldn't yet see.

Darwin and Seraphina now attend the same college, where their relationship has become the talk of the campus. Unlike fleeting romances, theirs is recognized as something profound and unwavering.

They are inseparable—whether in the lecture halls, the library, or during late-night study sessions under the stars. Darwin and Seraphina have found a home in each other—a love that feels both natural and extraordinary, as if the universe had always meant for their paths to cross. Their story isn't over; it's only just beginning, unfolding with each moment they create together.

6

It was just another usual day for Seraphina and Darwen. They had settled into their new routine, living together in their small studio apartment. Classes, meals, sleep—they did everything together. They were so comfortable around each other, it felt like they were one person, sharing every moment, every thought.

One afternoon, after class, Seraphina suddenly got a craving for something sour. "I need sour candies," she said, looking at Darwen with wide eyes. Before he could even respond, she switched to another craving, and then another. "What's going on with me?" she muttered.

Darwen, chuckling, teased her, "Look at you. You're craving like a pregnant woman! You know, that's a thing. Pregnant women crave sour stuff."

The words hit her like a thunderclap. "Darwen... take me to the hospital," she said, her voice serious. Darwen froze, confused. "What? Why?"

"Just take me, please!" she insisted, her urgency growing.

They headed to the hospital, and as soon as they arrived, Seraphina rushed to see the doctor. "Can you tell me if I'm pregnant?" she asked, her heart pounding. The doctor ran some tests, and not long after, the results came back.

She was pregnant.

Walking out of the hospital, Seraphina held the reports in her hands. Darwen was waiting outside, a mix of emotions on his face. When she showed him the paper, he pulled her into a tight hug. "We're going to be parents," he whispered, his voice full of love and disbelief.

But Seraphina pulled back slightly, her face uncertain. "Darwen, I'm happy... but isn't it too soon? I wanted to be a mom one day, but I don't have a job, no money... What am I supposed to do? I want to give my kids the best life."

Darwen cupped her face in his hands, looking her straight in the eyes. "Seraphina, I'm going to work. I'll work for you and the baby. I have the money, you don't need to worry. I'll take care of you both." He kissed her forehead, and his words gave her a sense of peace she hadn't expected.

Seraphina's face lit up with joy. "It's going to be so much fun," she laughed, her excitement bubbling over.

From that moment, their lives were turned upside down. They dropped out of college—neither of them liked it anyway. Darwen's dad owned a business, and Darwen was determined to take over and run it. "I'm going to take care of everything, Sera. You can 100% depend on me," Darwen reassured her with confidence.

Though their apartment was small, it was home, and it was theirs. But one day, Seraphina tried calling her mom, Nina, who lived in Cloverfield. She called several times, but there was no answer. It was strange. Her mom always answered.

Worried, Seraphina sent a text: *"Mom, I'm pregnant."*

The reply came the next day, and it crushed her heart. *"What do you mean you're pregnant? I spent all that money on your future, and you're out there making these mistakes? I hate you. Don't contact me again. Goodbye."*

Seraphina's world shattered. She'd never expected this from her mom. She collapsed into tears, her body shaking with sobs.

Darwen held her close, whispering soothing words. "It's okay, Sera. I'm here for you. I already told my parents, and they're happy for us. They might not be able to meet us now, but they're thrilled. And once you give birth, we'll go to Cloverfield and see your mom. Maybe when she sees her grandkids, she'll come around."

Seraphina wiped her eyes and nodded. "You're right. I hope so."

Then, Darwen gently pulled away from her, his eyes filled with a deep, unwavering love. He dropped to one knee, looking up at her with a soft, but sincere smile.

"Sera, my love," he began, his voice shaking slightly with emotion. "Will you marry me?"

Tears filled Seraphina's eyes as her heart raced. She had never expected this moment, but it felt so right. She reached out, cupping his face in her hands, as he held her gaze, waiting for her answer.

"Yes... yes, of course!" she whispered, her voice breaking.

Darwen smiled through his tears, pulling her close again, their hearts beating in sync as they shared an intimate moment of joy and promise.

It was the beginning of something beautiful.

With Darwen working hard to support them, and her friends offering their love and support, Seraphina carried on. And then, one day, the moment came. Seraphina gave birth—not to one, but two beautiful babies: twins, Catherine and Ethan.

Instead of tears, Seraphina laughed, her heart full of happiness. She was a mother now, and she was ready for this new chapter. Darwen was right there beside her, smiling through his tears, as they embraced their new life together.

They were a family now. And no matter what came their way, they would face it, together.

24

7

It had been a year since Seraphina became a mom, and every day felt like a dream to her. With Darwen, her two beautiful kids, and their tiny, cozy family, her life was filled with joy and purpose. She often reflected on how life had surprised her—coming to study and instead finding what she truly loved and cherished.

But one thing weighed on her heart: her mother, Nina. The distance between them since her pregnancy was something Seraphina couldn't shake off. One quiet evening, as she sat with Darwen while the kids played on the carpet, she turned to him.

"Darwen, how about we go to Cloverfield to see my mom?" she asked, her voice tinged with hope. "It's been so long. I miss her, and I want to apologize. I know she'll forgive me."

Darwen's eyes softened as he reached for her hand. "Yes, Sera. I want you to feel happy. Let's go to Cloverfield. When do you want to go?"

Seraphina's face lit up. "Well, it's New Year's in just a few days, and I have an idea.Let's go to Rosewyn first, it is a place in mistwood. It's the place where New Year is celebrated in such a grand way. And, Darwen," she added with a smile, "it's your birthday on New Year's Day. Let's celebrate all together with the kids. It'll be our first New Year as a family.

Then, right after that, we'll head to Cloverfield to see my mom. How does that sound?"

Darwen grinned, his love for her shining through. "Whoa, that's an amazing idea. We get to celebrate with the kids, and it'll be perfect. When did my wifey become so smart?" He pulled her closer, locking her in his arms, and teased her lovingly.

Seraphina laughed, resting her head on his shoulder. "I've always been this smart. You're just noticing now." They both laughed, looking over at their kids, who had fallen asleep on the floor, and soon, they joined them, drifting into a peaceful sleep as a family.

On December 31st, they packed up and left for Mistwood. Mistwood, part of their country Vaeloria, was known for its serene beauty and grand New Year celebrations. The journey from Silverbay to Mistwood was breathtaking, with snow-dusted forests and mountains lining the way. As they approached Mistwood, Seraphina stared out the window, her eyes misty.

"Wow," she whispered. "I don't know why, but this place is giving me such nostalgia. It's making me emotional, but I know I've never been here before."

Darwen glanced at her with a gentle smile. "It happens. Maybe you're connected to this place in some way. Who knows?"

They arrived at their hotel just as the sun began to set, painting the sky in hues of orange and purple. After settling in, Seraphina turned to Darwen.

"Babe, I'm going out for a bit of shopping. Just take care of the kids, and I'll be back soon. After that, let's watch the fireworks together."

Darwen raised an eyebrow. "Let me come with you."

Seraphina shook her head, smiling mischievously. "No, no. I have some plans, and I want to surprise you. So please, stay here."

Darwen sighed playfully. "Alright, go. But don't take too long."

She kissed him on the cheek, grabbed her bag, and left with a bounce in her step. Walking through the cozy streets of Mistwood, Seraphina felt a mix of excitement and nostalgia. The air was crisp, filled with the scent of pine and baked goods. She stopped by a quaint cake shop, her eyes scanning for the perfect cake to celebrate Darwen's birthday and their family's first New Year together.

Finally, she found it—a beautifully decorated cake with intricate designs of snowflakes and stars. As she carried the cake, she couldn't help but smile, imagining Darwen's reaction.

With her hands full of her purchases, she stepped outside and crossed the bustling road, heading toward the bridge that overlooked the river. The sun dipped low on the horizon, casting golden hues over the flowing water. As she walked onto the bridge, something caught her eye—a small box sitting inconspicuously on top of the railing. Intrigued, she bent down and picked it up. The box felt smooth and cold in her hands, and when she opened it, her breath hitched.

Inside were two exquisite rings, their designs intricate and timeless. They glimmered as though they had been crafted only yesterday, yet they carried an undeniable air of vintage charm. Sera slipped one onto her finger, the cool metal hugging her skin. She turned her hand, marveling at how perfectly it fit. Her heart swelled with curiosity and wonder.

"Sera... Seraphina, is that you?"

The voice startled her. She quickly placed the other ring and the box into her bag and turned around. Her eyes widened as she took in the figure before her.

"Morwen?" she breathed. "Hey... how have you been? It's been so long."

Standing there was Morwen, a boy she had known from her past. Back then, he had been quiet and shy. But now, he stood with an air of confidence that was almost unrecognizable.

Time and distance had changed him. Morwen was the twin brother of Darwen, but their bond was nonexistent—they were like distant strangers who never talked to each other, separated by unspoken walls of resentment and misunderstanding.

Morwen gave a small smile. "I'm back from abroad, just for a break and a party. It's good to see you, Sera."

"You too," she said softly.

He hesitated for a moment, then asked, "So, what are you doing here all alone? Are you here for a party as well?"

Sera nodded, her smile returning. "Yes, but this party is very special. I'm celebrating it with my family."

Morwen's face lit up with understanding. "Oh, so you're here with your parents?"

She shook her head, her voice steady yet warm. "No, Morwen. I'm here with Darwen and our kids, Ethan and Catherine."

For a moment, Morwen froze. The words hung in the air, heavy and unyielding. His expression shifted from surprise to something darker, something that made Sera's chest tighten. He looked at her with an intensity she had never seen before, and it made her uneasy.

"Oh... I see," he said finally, his voice barely above a whisper.

Sera sensed the change in him. "Well, it was nice seeing you again, Morwen," she said, her tone light but edged with discomfort. "Enjoy your party."

She turned to leave, but before she could take a step, Morwen's voice cut through the air, sharp and trembling with anger.

"What do you mean?" he shouted. "What the fuck do you mean, Sera?"

She froze, her heart pounding. Slowly, she turned back to face him. His face was contorted with rage, his eyes wild and unrecognizable.

"I worked and studied day and night for you," he spat, his voice rising with every word. "For you! And now you're here, having fun with that selfish bastard Darwen? I don't even call him my brother anymore! You don't deserve him, Sera. And now that you're with him, you've become just like him!"

Sera stepped back, her hands trembling. "Morwen, stop. You're scaring me."

But he didn't stop. His anger consumed him, blinding him to the fear in her eyes. He grabbed her shoulders, his grip tight and unforgiving.

"If I can't have you," he growled, his voice low and menacing, "then no one can."

Before she could react, he shoved her backward. Time seemed to slow as she stumbled, the edge of the bridge rushing toward her. She screamed, a piercing sound that echoed in the evening air, and then she was falling. The world blurred, the cold wind whipping against her skin as the river below grew closer.

The cold water shocked her system, numbing her senses. She struggled to stay afloat, her mind racing. She thought of Darwen, the kids, and the beautiful life they had built together.

Meanwhile, Morwen stood on the bridge, his chest heaving, his face a mask of twisted satisfaction and regret. His heart was filled with a mix of anger and horror.

He had never truly intended to hurt Seraphina, but in a moment of impulsive rage, he had made a terrible mistake. As he watched her disappear beneath the water's surface, a wave of regret and disbelief washed over him. Without another word, he turned and walked away, leaving the bridge empty and silent, yet haunted by what had just happened.

Darwen awoke with a start, his breath shallow and uneasy. The quiet hum of the hotel room was broken only by the soft, rhythmic sound of his children's breathing as they slept peacefully beside him. But something was wrong. He glanced at the clock on the nightstand—11:30 PM. A wave of panic surged through him. Seraphina was still not back from her shopping trip, and his heart skipped a beat.

He gently pulled the blanket over his children, ensuring they were safe, and without a second thought, he rushed to the hotel phone, calling the front desk. His words came out in a rush as he asked a staff member to watch over the kids. "I'll be back in a moment," he added hastily, though his voice trembled with uncertainty.

As Darwen left the room, the city outside was alive with energy. The streets of Mistwood were filled with people rushing in every direction, preparing for the upcoming celebrations. But for Darwen, none of it mattered. His mind was consumed with thoughts of Seraphina. He scanned the bustling crowd, searching for any sign of her, his heart pounding faster with each passing second.

His footsteps echoed through the streets as he moved from one shop to the next. The excitement in the air only made his fear grow stronger. He clutched a picture of Seraphina, desperate for someone to have seen her. At a small bakery, he approached the shopkeeper, his voice shaky. "Excuse me, ma'am," he said, showing her the photo. "Have you seen this woman?"

The lady peered at the photo, her face lighting up. "Oh, yes! She was here earlier this evening. She bought a beautiful cake and seemed so excited. She even mentioned something about watching the fireworks with her family."

Darwen's heart gave a flicker of hope. She was here. She was so close. Maybe she was still nearby. "Thank you," he murmured, turning on his heel, eager to continue his search.

His steps quickened, his pulse racing. He passed through the crowded streets, calling her name quietly but urgently. He finally reached the bridge near the town square and stopped dead in his tracks.

Seraphina's handbag.

It was abandoned on the bridge, surrounded by shopping bags. Darwen felt a cold grip on his chest, a sense of dread pulling him in.

"Seraphina?" he whispered, his voice catching in his throat. There was no answer, only the sound of distant chatter and the echo of his own footsteps.

He stepped forward, looking down into the river below. His eyes locked onto a familiar white scarf—Seraphina's scarf—stuck to a rock, the delicate flowers on it now stained with the dark waters. It was her scarf, the one she always wore. She had loved it, always kept it close, just like everything she had loved.

Without thinking, Darwen rushed down to the river, the cold water seeping into his shoes as he waded through it. His hands trembled as he reached out to grab the scarf, lifting it from the water, clutching it to his chest. He squeezed his eyes shut, but the tears still came, hot and uncontrollable.

And then, as the fireworks began to crackle in the distance, a single tear slipped down his cheek. Seraphina had always wanted to watch the fireworks with him, with their children. She had always wanted these moments. And now, here he was, alone with nothing but her scarf, the symbol of everything they had dreamed of.

A deafening boom from the fireworks shook the air above him. The bright colors that lit the sky only made the emptiness inside him deeper. Darwen fell to his knees on the riverbank, sobbing uncontrollably. He couldn't breathe. He couldn't think. All the plans they had made, the life they had built together, had shattered in an instant.

He clutched the scarf harder, feeling the last connection to her slipping away. He couldn't let go, not yet. He stood shakily, his hands clenched into fists, and made his way back to the bridge, his heart pounding in his chest.

He needed answers. He had to know what had happened to her. He glanced around the bridge and saw a small shop nearby with a CCTV camera above the door. Without thinking, Darwen rushed inside, nearly desperate.

"Excuse me, sir," Darwen said, his voice shaking, "Can I please see your CCTV footage? My wife is missing. I need to know where she is."

The shopkeeper paused for a moment, studying Darwen's face. But then, after a long sigh, he agreed. "Alright, I'll show you," he said, leading Darwen to the back of the shop.

The footage flickered on the screen. Darwen's breath caught in his throat. The camera caught a figure in the distance, his twin brother, **Morwen.** He watched, frozen in shock, as Morwen grabbed Seraphina and shoved her into the river without a second thought.

His hands shook as the reality set in. He stared at the screen, not wanting to believe it, but knowing it was true. Morwen—his brother, his flesh and blood—had pushed his wife into the freezing water.

The shopkeeper looked at him, his voice heavy with disbelief. "Do you know this man? He looks just like you."

Darwen could barely speak. The words stuck in his throat, thick and painful. "Yes. He's my twin brother," he whispered hoarsely, tears streaming down his face. "I don't know why he did it... I don't understand. He pushed my wife."

The shopkeeper shook his head gravely. "I'm sorry, but the river flows fast. With how cold the water is, and with the rocks below... it's unlikely she survived."

Darwen's knees gave way, and he collapsed into a chair, his hands gripping the sides of the table as his world shattered into pieces. **Seraphina was gone.** The woman he had promised to love forever, the mother of his children, was taken from him in the cruelest way.

He left the shop and immediately reported the crime to the police. The officers began their search, but Darwen couldn't shake the feeling that he was losing her forever.

Soon, they found Morwen, drunk and stumbling inside a bar not far from the bridge. Darwen followed them, rage coursing through his veins. When they reached Morwen, Darwen was overcome with fury. Without a word, he lunged at his brother, grabbing him by the collar.

"What the hell did you do?" Darwen shouted, his voice breaking. "What did you do to my wife? How could you? How could you hurt her like that?"

Morwen shoved him back, his face twisted in anger. "You don't get it, do you?" he spat. "You've always had everything! Everyone loved you—everyone thought you were perfect. I was always in your shadow. And now you've even got the woman I wanted! She was mine too!"

The two brothers fought fiercely, their emotions boiling over in a mess of anger, betrayal, and pain. But then, suddenly, it fell silent. The officers stepped in and restrained Morwen, arresting him and taking him away.

Darwen stood there, shaking. His body felt hollow, as if something had been ripped away from him. He turned to the officers, pleading, "Please... find my Seraphina. Please tell me she's still alive. You have to find her."

The officer looked at him sadly. "I'm sorry, sir. The water's cold, and the current is fast. There's a chance, but it's slim. I don't want to give you false hope."

Darwen's heart cracked. His mind screamed against the officer's words, but he couldn't argue. His wife was gone, and there was nothing he could do to bring her back.

That night, as Darwen lay awake in the hotel room, the weight of everything that had happened settled over him like a suffocating blanket. The silence of the room was deafening. The clock ticked away, marking the passing of time that no longer held any meaning.

He thought about Seraphina's words, the ones she had said in Mistwood when they first arrived: "I don't know why, but this place is giving me such nostalgia. It's making me emotional, but I know I've never been here before."He had told her then, "Maybe it's fate. Something might be connected to you here." Now, he wasn't sure if it was fate or something darker, but all that remained was the painful knowledge that she was gone.

His tears fell freely as he thought about their life together—the laughter, the love, the small moments that had meant everything. But now, with his heart shattered, he only had memories.

Suddenly, the sound of little feet padded across the room. Catherine, their one-year-old daughter, reached up and called out softly, "Dada," her tiny voice so full of innocence. She kissed his cheek, her first words.

Darwen felt something stir within him—a flicker of strength. His heart was still broken, but he realized he couldn't give up. Not now. For Seraphina, for their children, for the life they had dreamed of together. He wiped his eyes, kissed his daughter's head, and whispered softly, "I'll live for you. I'll live for both of you."

But then, a thought struck him—Seraphina's mother. Seraphina had always loved her mom, often speaking fondly of her. Darwen knew he had to tell her what had happened, but the painful truth was, he didn't know where Cloverfield was or how to find her.

Feeling the weight of this regret, Darwen realized he couldn't go to Cloverfield. He didn't even know where Seraphina's mother lived. With a heavy heart, he made the decision to go back to Silverbay. He had his children to care for, and that's where he needed to be.

9

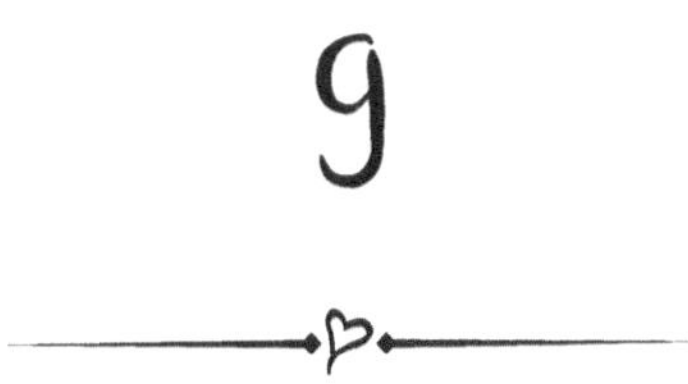

Morwen sat alone in his prison cell. The days felt like years. He stared at the same gray walls, watched the same guards walk past, and heard the same sounds day after day. It was the same routine, and he was so bored, so angry. This place is hell, he thought, grinding his teeth. He had no one to talk to, nothing to do, and no regrets about what he had done. Pushing Seraphina into the river? He didn't care. He didn't care about anything anymore.

Then, one day, he noticed her.

Olly.

She was walking down the corridor with a tray of food, her head down, her expression unreadable. Morwen's eyes followed her, and for the first time in a long while, something in his chest stirred. She glanced up and met his gaze. For a second, neither of them moved, just staring at each other. Her eyes were soft, but there was something sharp about them too. Why is she looking at me? Morwen thought, his heart racing a little.

She quickly turned away, continuing her rounds. But Morwen couldn't shake the feeling that something had just changed.

Days passed, and Olly kept coming back. Every time she did, Morwen couldn't help but watch her. She always kept her distance, never saying anything to him, but there was something about the way she looked at him. Does she feel it too? he wondered.

One day, as she handed him his lunch, he couldn't resist anymore. "You know," he said with a grin, "it's not so bad here when I get to see you." His voice was low, almost teasing, but there was a hint of something more—something desperate.

Olly didn't look up immediately, but her lips twitched. "You shouldn't talk to prisoners," she replied quietly, her voice steady but not cold.

Morwen laughed. "And yet, here you are. Talking to me."

There was a moment of silence before she spoke again. "Why are you still here? Don't you hate it?"

"Yeah," Morwen said, leaning back, trying to act casual. "But I wouldn't survive without something to look at. I think I like looking at you."

For the first time, Olly's face faltered. A flicker of something passed through her eyes—was it sadness?

"What's wrong?" Morwen asked, his voice softening. "You look upset."

She quickly shook her head. "It's nothing," she said. "I've just got my own problems."

Morwen nodded, though a part of him didn't believe her. "Yeah, everyone has their problems," he said, his tone serious for a moment. "But it's nice to talk, right? Makes this place a little less... boring."

And so, it started. Every day, they found themselves talking. At first, it was just small things, quick exchanges. But then it grew. Olly would smile at him when she handed him his food, and Morwen began looking forward to her visits, the only time he didn't feel like he was completely losing himself.

One night, when the prison was silent, Olly sneaked into Morwen's cell. The tension between them was palpable, their breaths shallow and hurried. They didn't speak much. It was just... an understanding. They needed each other in that moment, and in the quiet of the night, they made love.

It wasn't just physical; it was something deeper, something they both craved in this cruel, unforgiving world. They both knew the risks, but for that brief moment, it didn't matter. For the first time, they felt alive.

After that night, their bond grew stronger. During the day, Olly would pass by his cell, and their eyes would meet, filled with secrets only they knew. At night, when the prison fell silent, they would steal moments together, whispering dreams of freedom and a life far away from the cold, gray walls.

Then, one day, Olly approached him, her eyes serious. "Morwen," she said, her voice low, "didn't you say this place felt like hell? Didn't you say you wanted to get out of here?"

Morwen looked at her, his heart pounding. "Yeah, I've been wanting out for a long time."

She paused, looking around to make sure no one was near. "What if I could help you get out? What if we could escape?"

For the first time in his life, Morwen felt something close to hope stir inside him. He couldn't believe what he was hearing. "You would help me?" he asked, his voice raw.

Olly nodded, her eyes fierce. "I can get you out. Nobody's going to be awake at 2 a.m., and I have a pass to check in and out of the prison."

Morwen's heart raced, but then something else happened. Olly reached into her pocket and handed him a piece of paper. A report. The words on it made his breath catch in his throat.

"I'm pregnant," Olly whispered, her voice barely audible.

Morwen felt his heart shatter. For a moment, he couldn't breathe. He thought about his past, the things he had done. He had killed someone. He had been cold. He had hurt people. And now, here was this woman, pregnant with his child, ready to help him escape. I can't believe this is happening.

"I love you," Morwen whispered, the words slipping out before he could stop them.

Olly smiled, her eyes softening. "I know. And I love you too."

It was time. At 2 AM, Olly quietly opened the prison door. They crept out, their hearts pounding, both terrified but determined. The night was their only chance. Olly led Morwen through the dark corridors, and then they were out—free.

They ran.

Olly took Morwen to a new place, far from the city, far from anyone who knew them. It was in the woods, isolated, where no one would come looking for them. There, in that small, hidden house they built together, they began their new life.

Morwen went into town occasionally, always wearing a hat and trying to blend in. He bought food and supplies, doing whatever he could to keep them hidden. Days turned into weeks, weeks into months, and life felt almost peaceful for the first time in a long time.

One evening, while they were sitting by the fire, Morwen asked Olly about her past.

"My parents... they don't exist," she said, her voice distant. "I loved them, but they never loved me. They made me work, even when I was a child. So, I ran away with all their money."

Morwen listened, feeling a deep sympathy for her. He had his own broken past, but Olly's was different. It made him want to protect her, to take care of her.

"I will take care of you and our child," he promised, his voice firm. "I'll never leave you."

Months passed, and Olly's pregnancy grew harder. One night, she cried out in pain, and Morwen rushed to her side. He had never been a doctor, but he knew a little from his time as a student. As the pain grew worse, he knew it was time.

Olly gripped his hand, her face pale, tears streaming down her cheeks. "I'm scared," she whispered. "But I'm ready, Morwen. I'm ready to meet our baby."

With all his strength, Morwen helped her through the birth. When the baby was finally born, Morwen held him in his arms, looking at the tiny boy with tears in his eyes. He's ours.

"Look, Olly," Morwen said, his voice choked with emotion. "He's our son. He's perfect."

But when he looked up at Olly, she was motionless, her eyes closed. He checked her pulse, his heart sinking as he realized she was gone.

"No! No, please!" he screamed, shaking her. But it was too late.

Olly had died giving birth to their son.

The world felt like it had shattered in that moment. She was gone, and he was left holding their child, alone. For the first time, he understood the pain his brother Darwen must have felt. He had taken Seraphina's life, and now Olly was gone. He had killed Seraphina, and now this was his punishment. Karma had caught up with him.

He cried, truly cried, for the first time in his life.

Morwen couldn't take her to a hospital— if he did, he'd be caught, and his son would be at risk, But he couldn't leave her like this. With trembling hands, he dug a small grave in the woods and buried her there, his tears mixing with the dirt.

Now, it was just him and his son. Alone in the woods, living the life they had carved out.

But one day, while playing with the boy, Morwen noticed something that froze his heart. His son didn't seem to be looking at the toys Morwen had bought.

"Baby?" Morwen whispered. "Can you see?"

But there was no response.

His son... was blind.

And in that moment, the weight of everything hit him again. Morwen had thought he was free, but life had a way of reminding him—reminding him that nothing comes easy, and nothing is ever really simple.

He held his son tighter, tears brimming in his eyes. I will protect you, he promised. I will never let you feel alone like I did.

10

Morwen paced the small room where he had been hiding with his son. His heart ached as he looked at the boy—his tiny hands clutching his blanket, his unseeing eyes staring into nothing. The boy was blind, and Morwen felt helpless. He had been many things in his life—reckless, ruthless, even a criminal—but seeing his child like this, so innocent and vulnerable, made him feel something new. A determination.

I have to do something.

That evening, he made a decision. Covering his face with a scarf and pulling a hat low over his eyes, Morwen picked up his son and made his way to the nearest hospital. Every step he took was filled with fear. The police were always looking for him. But this wasn't about him anymore. It was about his son.

Inside the hospital, Morwen hesitated at the front desk, his voice low. "I… I need a doctor to look at my son," he said, holding the boy close.

The receptionist barely looked up. "Room 203. Third floor. Wait there."

Morwen nodded and hurried to the room. The doctor, a kind-looking woman with glasses perched on her nose, glanced at him briefly before focusing on the boy.

"What seems to be the problem?" she asked, lifting the boy gently from Morwen's arms.

"He… he can't see," Morwen said, his voice almost breaking. "Please, do something. Help him."

The doctor examined the boy carefully, checking his eyes and asking a few questions. After a while, she looked up at Morwen and smiled softly.

"It's temporary blindness," she said. "It can be corrected with a simple surgery. It won't take long."

Morwen felt a wave of relief wash over him. His knees almost buckled, and he had to steady himself against the wall. "Thank you," he whispered. "Thank you so much."

The doctor smiled again. "You can bring him tomorrow morning. Early. We'll get it done."

Morwen nodded quickly. "I'll be here."

The doctor hesitated. "We'll need some details for the records. What's the child's mother's name?"

Morwen froze. His mind raced. "What do I say?" He took a deep breath. *Nobody's going to know Olly is gone. Just say it.*

"Olly," he said, his voice steady. "Her name is Olly."

The doctor scribbled on her notepad. "And your name?"

Again, Morwen hesitated. "Mo… Morwen," he said finally.

The doctor looked at him, slightly suspicious but not questioning him further. "And the child's name?"

This time, the pause stretched longer. His heart sank. The truth was, he had never named the boy. He was always just Baby to him.

"His name is…" Morwen paused. He blurted, "Baby. His name is Baby."

The doctor raised an eyebrow but wrote it down anyway. "Alright, Mr. Morwen," she said, her tone curious. "We'll see you tomorrow."

As he turned to leave, she asked one last question. "Why are you wearing a mask?"

Morwen stammered. "Ah... oh, this? I have a cold. I didn't want my son to catch it."

The doctor gave him a polite nod, though she didn't seem entirely convinced.

The next morning, Morwen arrived early at the hospital, clutching his son tightly. The boy looked up at him, unable to see but somehow sensing his father's nervousness.

"It's going to be okay," Morwen whispered, pressing a kiss to the boy's forehead. "You'll see the world soon."

The nurse approached with a kind smile and led them inside. "We'll take good care of him," she said, gently taking the boy from Morwen's arms.

Morwen watched as his son was carried away, his heart heavy with both hope and fear. He was directed to the waiting room, where he sat, restless.

Minutes turned into hours. Morwen paced the room, glancing nervously toward the surgery doors. His mouth felt dry, so he walked over to the water dispenser, lowered his mask, and took a sip.

It was then that a man sitting nearby looked up, his eyes widening. "That's him!" the man whispered urgently to a security guard. "He's the wanted guy! I saw his face on the news!"

Within minutes, police officers entered the hospital quietly. They spotted Morwen, slowly approaching him from behind.

"Hands up!" one of them shouted, pointing a gun.

Morwen froze, his heart sinking. He raised his hands, turning to face them.

"Please," he said, his voice trembling. "My son is in surgery. He needs me. Don't take me now. Please!"

The officers ignored his pleas, dragging him out of the waiting room. Morwen's cries echoed through the hospital corridors. "Don't do this! My son needs me!"

Meanwhile, a man entered the hospital, his face covered with a mask. It was Orsino, the famous magician and the son of Magnus, a wealthy scientist. He had come to pick up medicine but decided to sit in the waiting room as the hospital was crowded.

A nurse, beaming with joy, walked up to him with a baby in her arms. "Congratulations, sir! Your son's surgery was successful!"

Orsino stood, stunned. "What?"

The baby opened his eyes for the first time, looking directly at Orsino and smiling. Instinctively, Orsino reached out, his heart overwhelmed by the innocence and warmth of the moment.

The nurse handed him the baby, and for a brief moment, Orsino felt something he hadn't felt in years—pure, unfiltered joy.

"Wait," the doctor hurried over, her eyes wide. "Oh, I'm sorry, sir. There's been a mistake! He's not the father."

Orsino blinked, holding the baby, and removed his mask. "What do you mean?" he asked, his voice tense.

The nurse gasped. "Oh my goodness! You're Orsino! The magician! I'm such a big fan. I thought you were the dad because the real dad was also wearing a mask, and you were sitting in the same spot!"

The doctor frowned. "The man seemed suspicious to me. The police took him into custody earlier today. I think he might have kidnapped this baby."

Hearing this, Orsino's gaze softened as he looked back at the baby. "Kidnapped?"

The doctor nodded. "He was hesitant when I asked him questions. He said the baby's name was... Baby. It didn't feel right."

The nurse chimed in, "But we need a blood donor for the baby. He has a rare blood type."

Orsino glanced at the report in the doctor's hands. "I... I have this blood type. Let me donate."

The doctors were shocked but quickly prepared him for the procedure. As Orsino lay on the bed, his eyes remained fixed on the baby, who was placed on a nearby bed. The child smiled at him, and Orsino smiled back instinctively.

While blood was being drawn, Orsino asked the doctor, "What about the mother? Where is she?"

The doctor paused. "The man said her name was Olly."

Orsino bolted upright, his heart pounding. "Olly?"

"Yes," the doctor said, confused. "Why? Do you know her?"

Orsino's voice trembled as memories flooded back. "She... she was the love of my life."

He remembered her laughter, the sparkle in her eyes, and the promises they made. But most of all, he remembered the pain—when she vanished without a word, leaving him with nothing but questions and an ache that never healed.

His words hung in the air, heavy with emotion, as the past began to unravel before his eyes.

11

ORSINO'S PAST - CHILDHOOD

Orsino's memories felt like a haunting fog, clouding his mind with pain. He could still hear the sound of his mother's laughter, the joy in his sister's voice. But those were all gone now, swallowed by the depths of the ocean that had torn their world apart.

Orsino was the son of Magnus, one of the world's most brilliant scientists, a man who had a reputation not just for his intelligence but for his love for his family. Orsino's family had always been full of life, love, and laughter. They had everything they could ever ask for: wealth, status, respect, and each other. Magnus was a proud father, his daughter the apple of his eye and Orsino, the thoughtful and introspective son, who always stayed out of the spotlight but never lacked his own sense of purpose." They were a family bound by love and the promise of a bright future.

But all of that changed the day they decided to go on a vacation.

It was supposed to be a perfect trip, a time to get away from the pressures of their everyday lives. They planned to visit the vast ocean that lay between Cloverfield and

Mistwood, the biggest, most mysterious body of water they had ever seen. The weather was ideal, the skies clear and sunny, a perfect day for an adventure. Magnus's daughter was especially excited—this was her first time seeing the ocean, and she couldn't wait to experience it.

"Let's go, Dad! Let's race on the boat!" she squealed as she tugged at Magnus's sleeve, her eyes wide with anticipation.

"Please, please, let's do it!" she added, looking over at Orsino with a mischievous grin.

Magnus chuckled, his face lighting up with affection for his daughter. "Alright, alright, let's do it," he agreed, knowing that her happiness meant everything to him.

"Alright, we'll have two boats. Me and Orsino in one, and you and your mother in the other. Let's see who can get further," Magnus said with a smile.

Orsino, who wasn't as eager as his sister, hesitated. "Dad... I'm afraid," he said, his voice barely above a whisper.

But Magnus just smiled and gave him a reassuring look. "Come on, Orsino. Look at your sister. She's braver than you. Show her what you're made of." His father's words echoed in his head, pushing him to take the plunge. Reluctantly, Orsino climbed into the boat with his father.

The race began, and for a while, it was thrilling. The boats zipped through the water, the roar of the engine and the spray of water in the air made everything feel alive. Orsino's sister and her mother laughed, calling out to them from the other boat. But then, the tides started to change.

The ocean's calm surface turned into something more dangerous. The waves began to rise, higher and higher, pushing against the boats. Orsino could see his sister and mother struggling with their boat as it was caught in the rising tide. Their boat wasn't moving as fast anymore, the engine sputtering. His sister, ever the brave one, shouted back, "Mom! Let's keep going!"

But her mother, who was more cautious, looked around, sensing the change in the air. "Wait, honey," she said, her voice tight with concern. "The weather's getting bad." They both tried to tie their scarves around their necks for protection, the wind growing fiercer by the second. His sister wore a white scarf, her mother's a blue one.

Suddenly, a sharp gust of wind tore through the air. Orsino saw it—his mother's scarf, the one she wore that day, caught by the wind and ripped from her neck. It fluttered through the air before floating toward the water, dancing like a ribbon caught in time. His mother reached out in a desperate attempt to grab it, Before anyone could react, the creature lunged, and in an instant, it engulfed her whole. Orsino froze, staring in horror as his mother was swallowed by the ocean, her screams drowned out by the roar of the waves.

"Mom!" Orsino's voice broke through the chaos, but there was nothing he could do. His father's face went pale with shock, his entire body stiffening. "No..." he whispered, his voice shaking as he turned to Orsino. With trembling hands, he closed Orsino's eyes, not wanting his son to see the terrible sight.

"Don't look, Orsino," Magnus said softly, his voice filled with sorrow. His hands lingered for a moment on Orsino's face, the weight of the moment pressing down on them both.

On the other hand, Orsino's sister, standing on the other boat, had collapsed. She had fallen to the floor of the boat, her body limp. She didn't scream or call for help—she simply fell, her head hitting the boat's surface with a sickening thud. Orsino could only stare in shock, unable to comprehend what was happening.

Magnus quickly drove the boat toward the shore, his heart racing. Orsino, still in shock, could barely process what was happening. His eyes stayed closed, but he could feel the rush of the wind, the salty spray of the ocean on his face, and his father's trembling hands at the wheel. As they reached the shore, Magnus stopped the boat and immediately hugged Orsino, his chest heaving with grief. "I'm so sorry... I couldn't save her... your mom," Magnus whispered, his voice thick with sorrow. They cried together, the storm of emotions too much to bear. But even amidst their sorrow, the waves were growing more furious, the storm more violent.

"I have to go get her," Magnus said, his voice strained but determined. "I'll save your sister. Don't be afraid, Orsino. Stay here. I'll come back for you."

Orsino's heart pounded in his chest, his body trembling with fear. "Don't go, Dad," he cried. "Please! It's too dangerous!"

But Magnus, his face set in a mask of determination, ignored the plea. He pushed the boat back into the water, despite the heavy rain and the rising tides that were threatening to swallow everything. Orsino watched helplessly as his father sped toward the horizon, the boat cutting through the furious waves.

The wind howled, the rain lashed against Orsino's skin as he stood on the shore, his heart in his throat. He wanted to run after his father, to stop him, but his legs wouldn't move. His whole body felt like it was frozen in place. The storm was a living, breathing thing, and Orsino feared the worst.

Magnus, undeterred by the storm, fought against the waves, pushing forward as the ocean raged around him. He screamed his daughter's name into the storm, his voice breaking with desperation. "Please... Please come back..." he shouted, his eyes scanning the churning water.

And then, he saw it. The boat that had once been carrying his daughter was no longer afloat. It had been flipped over, filled with water, its once sturdy frame now powerless against the fury of the sea. Shattered pieces of wood and debris floated aimlessly on the surface, scattered by the waves. His heart stopped as the full realization hit him—the boat had been swallowed whole by the ocean, taking everything with it.

He screamed again, his voice raw with anguish, and dove into the water. The waves battered against him, but he swam, desperation driving him. He cried out into the endless water, calling her name again, but there was no answer. Minutes felt like hours as Magnus swam through the chaos, but no matter how hard he searched, he couldn't find her. The ocean had taken her. There was nothing left but the endless expanse of water and the haunting memory of her laughter.

Magnus returned to the shore, his movements slow and lifeless, like a man who had lost everything. His eyes were empty, devoid of hope, as he guided the boat back to where Orsino stood, frozen on the shore.

As he pulled the boat up, his face crumpled, the weight of what had just happened crushing him. He collapsed to his knees, his voice a broken whisper as he looked at Orsino.

"I'm sorry," he sobbed, his body shaking with the force of his grief. "I couldn't save anyone. I couldn't save her. I couldn't save your mother... or your sister..."

Tears streamed down Magnus's face, and Orsino, his heart shattered, dropped to his knees beside him. The two of them held each other tightly, the storm around them nothing compared to the storm of emotions within. They cried together, their sorrow a deep, endless well that seemed to have no bottom. The sound of the ocean, once so calming, now felt like a cruel reminder of what had been lost.

12

When Magnus and Orsino returned to their once lively home, it no longer felt like home. It was as if the warmth and joy had evaporated, leaving behind only silence and shadows. The walls that had once echoed with laughter now stood as a reminder of what was lost. Magnus could still hear his daughter's giggles and his wife's soothing voice in the stillness, but they were only echoes, ghosts of a past he could never reclaim.

Orsino didn't speak. He didn't eat. He sat by the window every day, staring into the horizon as if waiting for his mother and sister to return. Magnus was shattered by the sight of his son, so young and innocent, drowning in a sea of grief. But Magnus himself was no better. The weight of losing his wife and daughter pressed on his chest like an anchor, pulling him deeper into despair.

Days turned into weeks, and nothing changed. Orsino didn't go to school, and Magnus didn't have the heart to tell him to. Every day felt like the same day—gray, heavy, and unending.

One evening, as the setting sun bathed their quiet home in orange hues, Magnus couldn't bear it anymore. He couldn't let his son slip further into this void. For Orsino's sake, he had to try to live again, even if it meant hiding his own pain.

"Orsino," Magnus called gently, forcing a smile onto his face. "Come here. I have something to show you."

Orsino turned slowly, his eyes dull and lifeless. He trudged over to his father, who crouched down and whispered, "I have a magic trick for you."

Magnus performed a simple illusion, making a coin disappear and reappear behind Orsino's ear. For the first time since that tragic day, a flicker of light returned to Orsino's face. He smiled—just a small one—but to Magnus, it was everything.

Encouraged, Magnus spent the following days teaching himself more magic tricks. Every evening, he performed for Orsino, who watched with wide-eyed wonder. Slowly, Orsino began to laugh again. Magnus treasured those moments, though his heart remained heavy.

One day, Magnus sat beside Orsino and asked, "Do you want to learn some magic tricks yourself? It's pretty cool, isn't it?"

Orsino's eyes lit up, and for the first time, his voice carried excitement. "Yes, Dad! I want to learn!"

From that day on, Magnus and Orsino practiced magic together. Orsino became so skilled that he began performing for the neighborhood kids. Their cheerful applause and praises lifted his spirits. "Wow, Orsino! That's amazing!" they would say, and Orsino would beam with pride. Magnus watched from afar, his chest tightening with a bittersweet ache.

As Orsino grew into his teenage years, Magnus surprised him with an incredible gift—an amusement park. "It's all yours," Magnus said, his voice tinged with emotion. "You can perform your magic tricks here, bring smiles to even more people."

Orsino was overwhelmed with happiness. He spent his days at the park, dazzling crowds with his tricks and making children laugh. It became his sanctuary, a place where joy bloomed despite the pain of the past.

But while Orsino found a new rhythm to his life, Magnus could not escape his grief. He remained haunted by memories of his wife and daughter. Late at night, when the world was asleep, Magnus would wander into his daughter's room. It was untouched, as if she might walk in at any moment.

One night, unable to hold back his emotions, Magnus sat on her bed and sobbed. His eyes landed on an old camera resting on the table. With trembling hands, he picked it up and began flipping through pictures. Each photo was a portal to a happier time—a birthday celebration, a family picnic, his daughter's mischievous grin.

Then a video began to play. Magnus wiped his tears and watched. In the video, his daughter was holding the camera, pointing it at him. "What do you want to be when you grow up, sweetheart?" Magnus asked in the video.

She looked up at her mother, who smiled lovingly. "Well, I want... I want to become a mom!" she declared, her voice filled with innocence.

Her mother laughed, and Magnus in the video chuckled too. "A mom? Why not something else?" he teased.

His daughter giggled. "I'll be the second-best mom in the whole universe!"

"Why second-best?" Magnus asked, raising an eyebrow.

"Because the first-best mom is mine," she replied, wrapping her arms around her mother and kissing her cheek. The laughter and love in the video were so vivid, so alive, that Magnus felt his heart shatter all over again.

As the video ended, Magnus set the camera down and whispered, "Love... It makes life beautiful. And memories... They're all I have now."

That night, Magnus walked into his lab, a place he once considered his sanctuary, now heavy with memories. The air felt colder, quieter, as though it, too, mourned with him. His eyes fell upon a dusty vintage box sitting on the corner shelf, untouched for years. It was his grandfather's, filled with precious remnants of a past long gone. Among the items inside was a small chunk of metal, aged yet gleaming faintly under the dim light. He picked it up, his hands trembling.

Magnus stood there, holding the metal, staring at it for what felt like an eternity. His mind drifted to the times his daughter would beg him to let her into the lab. Her eyes would light up with wonder as she imagined herself crafting miracles alongside him. "Please, Daddy, just one little experiment!" she'd say, her voice sweet and pleading. But he had always said no. It was too dangerous, he'd told her, even as her excitement tugged at his heart.

Now, that same heart ached with regret. "I should have let her," he muttered to himself, his voice barely audible. Tears welled up in his eyes as he thought of her, of the life she should have lived, the dreams she would never chase. His knees nearly buckled under the weight of his sorrow, but he steadied himself. This time, he would create something for her—something to honor the love she had left behind.

Magnus carefully set up his tools, his hands moving with purpose but his chest tightening with every motion. The sound of the metal being heated filled the room, a stark contrast to the silence of his grief. As he worked, images of his family flooded his mind: his daughter's mischievous smile, his wife's gentle laughter, Orsino's innocent eyes. They were all there with him in spirit, guiding him through the pain.

He shaped the metal with painstaking care, pouring every ounce of his love, his sorrow, and his memories into each stroke. When he finished, three rings sat before him—simple, unassuming, yet radiating an almost ethereal beauty. Magnus stared at them, his vision blurred by tears. They weren't just rings. They were pieces of his heart, molded into a tangible form.

Placing the rings into a small, ornate box, Magnus held it close to his chest, as if it held the essence of his wife and daughter. He climbed the stairs slowly, his legs heavy but his determination firm. When he reached Orsino's room, he found his son sitting quietly by the window, the same place he always sat, lost in thought.

"Orsino," Magnus called softly, his voice cracking under the weight of his emotions. Orsino turned, his eyes meeting his father's. "I made something for you."

Magnus sat beside his son and opened the box, revealing the rings. "These rings," he began, his voice quivering, "are symbols of love. They are for your mother, your sister... and for you." He paused, his throat tightening as he fought back tears. "Carry them with you, always. They'll remind you that love never truly leaves us. It stays... in the memories, in the little things, in us."

Orsino's hands trembled as he picked up one of the rings. His eyes glistened with unshed tears as he slipped it onto his finger. Then, without a word, he leaned into Magnus and wrapped his arms around him, holding on tightly, as though afraid to let go.

"Thank you, Dad," Orsino whispered, his voice barely audible but filled with emotion. Magnus closed his eyes, savoring the warmth of his son's embrace. It was a moment of connection, of healing, even if just a small step forward.

From that day on, Orsino carried the box with him wherever he went. To him, it wasn't just a box, and the rings weren't just metal. They were his family—their love, their laughter, their unbreakable bond. No matter how much life tried to take away, Orsino knew he carried their essence within him, forever.

Orsino grew to become a beacon of hope in Mistwood. Known as the youngest magician, he enchanted audiences with his tricks, but it was his kindness and warmth that truly captivated people.

Though Magnus still carried the weight of his loss, he found solace in watching his son shine. Together, they proved that even in the face of unimaginable pain, love could light the way forward.

13

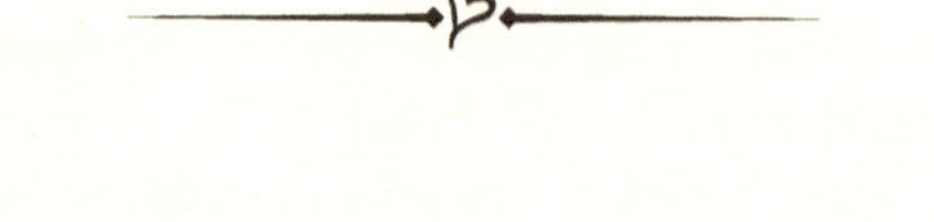

Years passed by, and Orsino had entered adulthood. Despite the passage of time, some things hadn't changed. Every evening, he went to the amusement park, where he felt a deep sense of purpose. Entertaining children with his magic tricks brought him joy, their laughter and wonder reminding him of why he did it. It wasn't about the tricks or the applause—it was the happiness he spread, and in return, he found his own. The park had become a sanctuary, a place where he could truly be himself.

The amusement park was quiet, its vibrant colors and lively sounds replaced by the peaceful hush of the night. Orsino had just finished another fulfilling day, bringing joy to kids with his magic tricks. This was his life—a life he loved. Watching the laughter and smiles of others filled the void in his heart, making the world seem a little brighter.

The children who had gathered earlier had all gone, leaving the place almost empty. Almost.

That's when he noticed her—a girl sitting on a bench, her posture relaxed yet hesitant. She was looking at him, her gaze steady, until their eyes met. Startled, she quickly looked away, her cheeks flushing as if caught in a secret. Orsino felt a pull, an unexplainable connection, like the universe had shifted slightly in that moment.

Without overthinking, he walked over and sat beside her, leaving a respectful gap. He turned to her, a gentle smile on his face, and broke the silence.

"So... how's life?"

She looked at him, startled at first, then smiled softly. "Here, at this moment, it's amazing. It's so peaceful," she said, her voice carrying a warmth that settled into Orsino's heart.

"I really like your magic tricks," she added, her tone genuine. "Where did you learn them?"

Orsino chuckled, slightly surprised. "Oh, really? My magic tricks usually impress kids. I didn't think someone like you would find them interesting too." He smiled wider, his boyish charm shining through. "I learned them from my dad."

She nodded thoughtfully, her gaze steady on him. "He must be really good."

"He is," Orsino replied with pride. "He's the reason I started doing all this."

They fell into a comfortable silence for a moment before he asked, "So, what's your dream?"

Her expression shifted, becoming wistful. She took a deep breath and smiled, her eyes reflecting the soft glow of the park's remaining lights. "My dream? To ride all these rides in the twilight, under the stars, with no crowd or noise. Just me... and the night sky."

Orsino paused, her words sinking into his heart. Then he asked, softly but with genuine curiosity, "What's your name?"

She hesitated, as if savoring the moment, then smiled. "Olly," she said simply.

He stood up immediately, his hand outstretched toward her. "Olly, let's go."

She looked up at him, puzzled. "Where?"

"To make your dream come true," he said simply, his eyes shining with excitement.

Her brows knitted in confusion, and she hesitated. "But isn't everything closed now? Everyone's gone. They won't operate the rides just for us."

He grinned, a playful glint in his eyes. "Don't worry. This is my amusement park. I can do whatever I want. Come on."

Her hesitation melted as she looked into his eyes—full of hope, determination, and something deeper she couldn't name. Slowly, she placed her hand in his, letting him guide her.

The night unfolded like a dream. The two of them rode every ride under the blanket of stars. The park, devoid of its usual bustle, felt like their own magical world. Laughter echoed in the stillness of the night as Olly's initial shyness gave way to pure joy.

Orsino watched her closely, mesmerized by the way her eyes lit up with each ride, her happiness contagious. For a moment, he forgot about everything—the pain, the loss, the loneliness. All he could see was her, and it felt like the universe had aligned just for this moment.

As the last ride slowed to a stop, Olly stepped off, her face glowing with a mix of exhilaration and emotion. She walked toward Orsino, her steps deliberate, and without a word, she hugged him tightly.

"Thank you," she whispered, her voice trembling. "Thank you so much for this. You didn't have to, but you did. You don't even know me, and yet..." She trailed off, her grip tightening around him. "You don't know how much I needed this."

Orsino stood still, overwhelmed by the sincerity in her words. And then, something shifted inside him. For the first time in years, he felt alive—truly, deeply alive.

As she pulled back from the hug, he found himself instinctively pulling her close again. They stood there, holding each other, no words exchanged, just an unspoken understanding that in that moment, they both needed this.

When Olly finally stepped back, her face was soft with gratitude. She leaned in, kissed him lightly on the cheek, and without another word, turned and ran.

Halfway down the path, she looked back, her eyes sparkling, and gave him a smile that took his breath away. Then she disappeared into the night.

Orsino stood frozen, his heart pounding, his cheeks flushed with a mix of shock and exhilaration. As the first drops of rain began to fall, he lifted his face to the sky, letting the cool water wash over him. He spread his arms wide and started dancing, the rain mingling with his laughter.

A car horn jolted him back to reality. Turning, he saw Magnus, his father, sitting in their old car with a bemused expression.

"Get in," Magnus called out, laughing.

Orsino, still smiling like a fool, ran to the car and climbed in.

Magnus raised an eyebrow, smirking. "Oh, I see someone was dancing in the rain. What's got you so happy?"

Blushing, Orsino stammered, "Oh, uh... well, Dad, it's just that—it rained after so long. I couldn't help it."

Magnus chuckled, shaking his head. "Whatever it is, I'm just glad to see you smiling."

They drove home, the rain tapping gently against the windows, while Orsino stared out, lost in thought. His heart was still racing, his mind replaying every moment of that magical night. For the first time in a long time, it felt like life was offering him something new—a spark, a hope, a connection.

Under the soft glow of moonlight filtering through his window, Orsino lay in bed, his heart warm with newfound joy. On his bedside table rested the magical rings, shimmering faintly in the dim light, as if they too felt his happiness. He picked one up, tracing its intricate patterns with his fingers.

"I think I've found it," he whispered to the ring, a smile spreading across his face. "I've found love, and it's... indescribable." His eyes glistened as he placed the ring back beside its companion and closed his eyes, anticipation painting dreams of Olly. Tomorrow seemed too far away.

The morning arrived with the chirping of birds, their melodies filling the air as Orsino prepared for his day at the amusement park.Orsino arrived early at the amusement park, his steps light and his heart hopeful. He carried his small bag of magic tricks, ready to perform for children and adults alike, but deep inside, he was eagerly waiting for one face—hers.

As the hours passed, the park buzzed with laughter and chatter. Orsino performed his tricks, occasionally glancing toward the entrance. Evening fell, and the laughter faded as the visitors slowly began to leave. Orsino's heart sank when the park was nearly empty, and Olly was nowhere to be seen.

Still, he waited. Hours passed, and the park grew silent, the once-bustling rides now still. Under the canopy of stars, Orsino finally made his way home, whispering to himself, She'll come tomorrow.

But the next day brought the same story, and the next, and the next. Days turned into a week, and each evening, Orsino stood near the carousel, scanning the crowd with hopeful eyes. The once-vivid anticipation now mingled with worry. Where was she? Was she safe? The questions gnawed at his mind, but his heart clung to hope.

Finally, on the seventh night, as Orsino prepared to leave, defeated and heartbroken, she appeared. Her silhouette against the soft glow of carousel lights stopped him in his tracks. It was her—Olly. Her face looked pale, her eyes puffy and red. The moment their eyes met, Orsino didn't think twice. He ran toward her and enveloped her in a tight hug. She broke down in his arms, her body trembling as she sobbed uncontrollably. He held her without saying a word, letting her cry as much as she needed. He wanted to ask her what was wrong, but he knew this wasn't the time. She needed comfort, not questions.

After a while, he gently led her to the carousel. The soft music played as it began to move, the horses bobbing up and down. Olly sat on one horse, and Orsino on another beside her. She wiped her tears and finally looked at him. "I missed you," she whispered. "I'm sorry I didn't come."

"I missed you more," he replied softly, his voice filled with relief and warmth. "I was dying to see you. But... will you tell me what happened?"

Olly hesitated, her fingers nervously gripping the carousel pole. Then, with a deep breath, she began. "That night, after we spent time here... it was the happiest I've ever been. I felt alive. For the first time, I felt loved and cared for.

You made me feel like I mattered."

She paused, her voice breaking as she continued. "But when I went home, everything fell apart. My parents... they were furious. My mom slapped me and yelled at me, asking where I had been. She said, 'Who's going to cook dinner for us? We've been starving while you're out having fun. Who knows what you're doing out there?' She shoved me, and then they both left to eat dinner somewhere, leaving me alone."

Her voice trembled as she spoke. "That night, I felt so broken. I realized that this wasn't just one bad night—it was my whole life. They've never loved me, Orsino. They've only yelled, scolded, and treated me like I'm nothing. I wasn't sent to school to learn or grow; I was sent to work and serve them. Love... I've never known what it feels like. Until I met you."

Orsino listened intently, his heart aching with every word she said. He clenched his fists, trying to keep his emotions in check as she continued.

"I couldn't take it anymore. When they went out that night, I wrote them a letter. I told them, 'Mom, Dad, I've always loved you, even though you've never loved me. All I ever wanted was love, but I see now that you'll never give it to me. So, I'm leaving. I'm taking your money—not because I want it, but because I deserve something for all the pain you've caused me. Don't try to find me, or I'll report everything you've done to the authorities.'"

Tears streamed down her face as she finished. "I took their money and left. I found a small room to stay in and started working part-time jobs. But... I've been so alone, Orsino. I didn't know who else to turn to, so I came back here. To you."

Orsino's eyes filled with tears. "Olly," he said, his voice thick with emotion, "that's unimaginable. What they did to you... it's so wrong. You deserve justice. You should report them and make them pay for what they've done."

"No," she said firmly, shaking her head. "I can't. I still love them, Orsino. I don't want to hurt them, even after everything."

Orsino fell silent, struggling to understand her forgiveness. He reached out, taking her hand in his. The carousel continued to spin slowly, the soft music enveloping them.

"Olly," he said gently, "if you won't report them, then promise me one thing. Let me be your family. You can stay with me and my dad. I want to give you the love you've been missing."

Olly gave him a small, tearful smile. "I appreciate that more than you know, Orsino. But... I need time. I need space to heal. And I don't want to inconvenience your father."

"It wouldn't be an inconvenience," Orsino insisted. "But I understand. Just know that whenever you're ready, my door is always open for you."

She smiled through her tears, her eyes softening. "Thank you," she whispered. "Thank you for being there for me."

As the carousel continued to go round in a steady rhythm, Olly asked softly, "What about your mom? Why is it just you and your dad?"

Orsino's face clouded with pain. He hesitated before speaking. "There was... an accident. I lost my mom and my sister years ago. It's just been me and my dad since then."

Olly's heart broke at his words. "I'm so sorry, Orsino," she said, her voice trembling. "I didn't mean to bring up something so painful."

"It's okay," he said, forcing a small smile. "We all have our struggles. But you know what? Even with all the pain, there are still beautiful memories to hold onto."

They sat in silence for a moment, each lost in their thoughts, finding comfort in each other's presence.

15

The carousel slows to a gentle stop, the cheerful music fading into the quiet hum of the night. Orsino glances at Olly, a soft smile playing on his lips as he steps down and turns to offer her his hand. She takes it, his grip warm and steady.

Together, they walk a few steps away from the carousel. The park feels almost dreamlike, bathed in the soft glow of scattered streetlamps. Orsino spots an empty bench beneath a tree, its branches swaying lightly in the cool breeze, and gestures toward it.

"Let's sit for a moment," he says softly.

Olly nods, following his lead. As they sit down, the silence between them grows, not awkward but heavy with unspoken words. Orsino fidgets briefly, his fingers brushing against the wooden edge of the bench. Then, as if gathering every ounce of courage, he turns to her.

"Olly," he begins, his voice quiet, almost afraid to break the stillness. "Do you... love me?"

For a moment, Olly doesn't respond. Her gaze drops to her hands, fingers nervously twisting. The question lingers in the air, pressing against her chest like a weight she's been carrying for years. She takes a deep breath before finally looking up at him

"Orsino," she begins, her voice barely above a whisper, "I've spent my whole life trying to figure out what love is. But all I ever knew was what it wasn't. Love wasn't the yelling, the harsh words, or the silence so heavy it crushed you. It wasn't the feeling of never being enough, no matter how hard you tried. That was all I had. I didn't even know love could feel... different."

She looks down again, her hands trembling slightly in her lap. Orsino watches her, his heart aching as he waits.

"But when I met you... everything changed," she begins, her voice soft and filled with raw emotion. "You looked at me like I was someone worth knowing, someone worth... caring for. I didn't realize it at the time, but you showed me what love could be. You didn't ask for anything, didn't demand explanations, or make me feel small. You just... gave.

And that night at the amusement park, when I saw you entertaining the kids, putting in so much effort to make them happy—the way your face lit up when you saw their joy—it was so beautiful. When I saw you smile, I'd automatically smile too. It felt like... like I'd finally found something good, something real.

And then you barely knew me, but you still made my dream come true. I told you I wanted a night where it was just me and the rides, under the stars, and you didn't even hesitate. You didn't ask why it mattered to me; you just made it happen. And in that moment, you gave me something I didn't think I'd ever feel—joy. Pure, unfiltered joy. I looked at you that night and thought, Is this what love could be?"

A tear slips down her cheek as her words hang in the air, her emotions laid bare.

Her hands tighten around his, her eyes locking onto his as if trying to make him feel the depth of her words. "So yes, Orsino. I love you. I've loved you since that night when you showed me that love doesn't have to be loud or perfect. It can be gentle. It can be quiet. It can be... you. But..."

Her voice falters, and she takes a shaky breath before continuing. "I'm scared, Orsino. I've only ever known pain, and I never want to bring that into your life. You deserve so much—more than I know how to give. But I promise you this: I will try. Every single day, I'll try to bring you the peace and happiness you've brought to me. You're my happiness, Orsino. And I want to protect that with everything I have."

Orsino reaches for her hands, holding them firmly but tenderly. His thumbs brush over her knuckles, grounding her as he speaks. "Olly, I know your heart. I know how hard it is to let yourself believe in something good when all you've ever known is the opposite. But with you... I don't feel afraid. With you, I feel whole. And that's enough for me. You are enough."

Olly lets out a shaky laugh, tears slipping down her cheeks as she nods. Orsino smiles softly, leaning forward to wipe her tears with his thumb. His touch lingers, his hand moving to cup her cheek. His gaze holds hers, warm and steady, as if silently reassuring her that everything she feels is valid, that she's safe.

He reaches out, his hand moving gently to her waist, pulling her a little closer, almost instinctively. His fingers find their way to her face, tucking a stray strand of hair behind her ear. His touch is soft, filled with a warmth that wraps around her like a promise. Then, slowly, he cradles her face, his fingers brushing along her jawline, his thumb resting near her cheek, as if holding something delicate, something he cherishes deeply.

Olly's breath catches as Orsino's hand slips to the back of her neck, drawing her closer until there's no space between them. And then, with a softness that speaks more than words ever could, he kisses her. It's a kiss that starts slow, filled with tenderness and restraint, but soon deepens, each moment lingering, their heartbeats merging in the silence. The world around them fades, and it's as if their souls meet, intertwining in a dance that neither of them ever wants to end.

Time ceases to exist, and all they feel is the warmth of each other, the steady rhythm of their heartbeats, each beat a silent vow. In that moment, they are one, bound by something deeper than words, a love that fills the spaces where words fall short.

When they finally pull back, their foreheads resting against each other, Olly's eyes shimmer with unshed tears of happiness. She smiles softly, feeling a peace she's never known, a quiet joy that says everything she can't put into words.

Orsino whispers, his forehead against hers, "You're my peace too, Ollie. My home. And I'd spend every day making sure you feel it."

They sit there, wrapped in each other, knowing that in this one moment, they've found a love that neither of them thought they'd ever know.

16

The moon hung high, casting a soft silver glow over the quiet streets as Olly and Orsino left the amusement park. The night had been unforgettable, filled with love, emotional moments, and a connection that felt like a dream come to life. Orsino turned to her, his eyes warm and filled with a quiet affection.

"Stay with me tonight," he said gently, his voice a low murmur in the stillness.

Olly blinked, her cheeks flushing slightly. "At your place?" she asked, her voice hesitant yet curious.

He smiled, his dimples deepening. "Yes. You'll be safe there. Besides, I want you to meet my dad."

Though a part of her felt nervous, she nodded, unable to deny the warmth she felt in his presence. They drove in comfortable silence, the hum of the car's engine the only sound between them.

When they arrived at his home, her breath caught in her throat. It wasn't just a house—it was a grand mansion, the kind that seemed pulled straight from the pages of a fairytale. The sprawling estate was adorned with elegant lights, a perfectly manicured garden, and a long driveway flanked by towering trees. Workers moved gracefully across the grounds, each one nodding respectfully to Orsino as they passed.

"This… this is your home?" she asked, her voice barely above a whisper.

Orsino chuckled softly, scratching the back of his neck. "It's just a house," he said modestly, though the grandeur around them suggested otherwise.

As they entered, the warmth of the interior embraced them. Chandeliers sparkled overhead, and the scent of fresh flowers lingered in the air. A tall man with graying hair and a strong presence approached them.

"Dad," Orsino said, his voice light with affection. "I'd like you to meet someone."

Magnus, Orsino's father, looked at Olly with a kind smile, his eyes twinkling with curiosity. "And who might this be?" he asked.

"This is Olly," Orsino said, his voice filled with pride. "Dad, I've found my happiness. She's the one I love."

Magnus's eyes softened as he studied Olly. He stepped forward, extending his hand. "It's a pleasure to meet you, Olly. Any woman who can bring that light into my son's eyes is more than welcome here."

Olly blushed, taking his hand. "Thank you, sir. It's… an honor to meet you."

The three of them spent the evening talking over a lavish dinner. Magnus shared stories of Orsino's childhood, drawing laughter from them both. As Magnus looked at Olly, something about her reminded him of his daughter, who was no longer with them. He had only seen his daughter as a little girl and often wondered how she might have looked as a grown woman. In Olly, he caught glimpses of what he had longed to see—a young woman full of life, strength, and quiet grace. The memory stirred a bittersweet ache in his heart, but it also made him embrace the present moment with a newfound gratitude. For the first time in a long while, Olly felt a sense of belonging—a warmth she hadn't realized she'd been missing.

After dinner, Magnus smiled knowingly. "Well, I'll leave you two to enjoy the rest of your night. Live your lives to the fullest, and don't hold back."

Olly's cheeks turned crimson at his words, and Orsino chuckled, shaking his head. "Goodnight, Dad," he said, taking Olly's hand and leading her upstairs.

When they reached his room, Olly was struck again by the sheer opulence of his life. The room was massive, with high ceilings, ornate furniture, and a bed that looked like it belonged in a royal palace. But what caught her attention was the small, unassuming ring box on the table beside the lamp.

"What's that?" she asked, pointing to it.

Orsino walked over, picking up the box with care. He opened it to reveal two intricately carved rings, their designs simple yet stunning.

"These," he said, his voice softer now, "were carved by my dad. He made them for my mom and my sister. After they... passed, these rings became the only pieces of them I had left. They're my most precious treasures, my symbol of love and memory."

Olly's heart clenched at the vulnerability in his voice. She reached out, her fingers brushing over the rings. "They're beautiful," she whispered.

Orsino looked at her, his eyes searching hers. "You're my family now, Olly," he said quietly. "These rings—they're a reminder of the love I've lost, but also of the love I've found. With you."

The night stretched on, a symphony of whispered promises and unspoken words. They explored each other in ways they hadn't before, each touch and kiss a testament to their deepening bond. The rest was history, a memory etched into their hearts forever.

The days passed quickly, and in just two days, the New Year would arrive. Orsino suggested they visit Rosewyn, a tradition in the country of Vaeloria. Every year, people gathered in the magical town nestled within Mistwood to celebrate, and it felt like the perfect way to welcome the new year. They decided to go two days before, wanting to spend time together, enjoying the start of this new journey in their lives.

The drive to Rosewyn was filled with laughter and shared dreams. Orsino booked them a beautiful room in one of the town's cozy inns. That night, they shared more than just the space; they shared their hearts. The love between them grew even stronger, and as they lay together, tangled in each other's arms, it felt as though the world had stopped for them.

The next morning, Olly woke up with a sharp, nagging pain in her head. At first, she tried to ignore it, thinking it was just a headache. But as the minutes passed, it only grew worse, like a constant pressure building up inside her skull. She clenched her jaw, trying to push through it, but the pain was unbearable.

"Orsino," she whispered, her voice shaking, "something's wrong. My head... it's hurting so much."

His eyes shot open, panic flooding his face. "We're going to the hospital. Now."

At the hospital, the doctor ran a series of tests. Olly sat in the sterile room, her hands trembling as she waited for the results. When the doctor returned, her face was grave.

"I'm so sorry," she began gently. "The scans show you have a rare brain disease. It's in the last stage. I hate to tell you this, but... you have about a year to live."

The words hit Olly like a tidal wave. Her knees gave out, and she sank into a chair, her mind spinning. "No," she whispered, shaking her head. "There must be a mistake. There has to be a cure. Tell me what I can do!"

The doctor placed a comforting hand on her shoulder. "I wish there was something. But the disease is too advanced. I'm so sorry."

Olly's world crumbled around her. Every dream, every plan she'd made with Orsino seemed to shatter in an instant. She felt hollow, as though the life had been drained from her.

When she stepped out of the room, Orsino was waiting anxiously. "What did they say? Are you okay?"

Olly forced a smile, though her heart was breaking. "It's nothing serious," she lied, her voice barely steady. "Just a migraine."

He didn't press further, but she could see the concern in his eyes. Back at the hotel, Olly sat on the bed, her mind racing. She thought of Orsino, of his love for her, and of the pain he would feel if he knew the truth. She couldn't bear the thought of him suffering because of her.

Maybe I should leave, she thought. If I go now, it'll hurt him, but not as much as it would later. If I stay, he'll only fall deeper, and when I'm gone, it'll destroy him.

She couldn't let him go through that. The decision burned in her chest like fire.

"I need to go," she said, her voice breaking as she stood up. "I can't do this to you."

Orsino's eyes filled with confusion and worry. "What do you mean? Where are you going?"

"I need space," she whispered, her voice cracking. "I'm sorry, Orsino. I just... I can't."

He moved toward her, his hands reaching for hers. "If that's what you need, I'll respect it. But I'm not going anywhere. I'll be here. I'll wait for you, no matter what."

His words pierced her heart, but she couldn't let him see the truth. She couldn't let him suffer the way she would.He reached into his pocket and pulled out a small wooden box. With trembling hands, he opened it to reveal two delicate rings. They were symbols of his love, something he had kept close to his heart for years. Olly knew what they meant. She knew why they were so important to him.

"These rings," he said softly, his voice thick with emotion, "they're everything to me. But I want you to have them. They're a promise. When you're ready, when you've found peace, come back to me. I'll be waiting."

Tears welled up in Olly's eyes as she took the box, clutching it to her chest. She wanted to scream, to beg him to understand, but the words wouldn't come. All she could do was whisper through her sobs, "I'm so sorry... I'm so sorry..."

With a heavy heart, she turned and walked out, leaving behind not just the hotel, not just Orsino—but a part of her soul as well.

17

As Orsino stood in the doorway, watching Olly walk away, his heart felt like it was being torn apart. The world he had only just begun to find joy in seemed to shatter before it could fully take shape. Every step Olly took away from him felt like another thread unraveling in the fabric of his life. He thought of the moments they shared, the laughter, the quiet conversations, and the dreams they hadn't even begun to fulfill. It was as if life had cruelly dangled happiness in front of him only to snatch it away before he could hold onto it.

Orsino sank into a chair, his hands trembling as he gripped the edge of the table. "Why? Why does everything I love leave me?" he whispered to himself. The thought echoed in his mind like a haunting melody, one he couldn't escape.

Meanwhile, Olly walked briskly away, her heart as heavy as the steps she took. She clutched the small wooden box in her hand—the rings Orsino had entrusted her with. His words played over and over in her mind: "These rings are my promise. When you're ready, come back to me." She wanted to scream, to cry, to turn back and tell him everything. But she couldn't.

She found herself at a bridge overlooking a river. The water flowed gently beneath her, glimmering under the sunlight like a ribbon of liquid silver. She stopped and leaned on the railing, staring down at the current. "Life is so beautiful," she murmured to herself, her voice trembling. "And yet, I'm leaving it so soon."

Tears spilled down her cheeks as she placed the small box on the railing. She ran her fingers over the smooth wood, her heart aching with every touch. "I'm so sorry, Orsino," she whispered, her voice breaking. "I can never hurt you... and that's why I have to leave." She closed her eyes, took a deep breath, and walked away, leaving the box behind.

Back at the hotel, Orsino sat in silence, unable to bear the emptiness Olly had left behind. He grabbed his car keys and left, the thought of staying in that space unbearable. He drove aimlessly, not knowing where he was going, until he found himself near a familiar river. He parked his car and walked toward the water's edge, feeling a strange pull toward the serene yet haunting scene.

It was the same river Olly had stood by just moments before, though she was long gone now. A bridge loomed overhead, its structure casting shadows on the water below. Orsino sat near the riverbank, staring at the flowing current. It reminded him of the day the water had swallowed his mother and sister. "Beautiful and terrifying," he thought, his voice heavy with pain. The memories resurfaced like ghosts, each one sharper than the last.

He ran his fingers through his hair, his mind racing. "Why did Olly leave?" he asked himself. "What could she be going through that she can't share with me? Will she ever come back?"

The water rippled softly, its gentle sound mocking the chaos in his mind. He sat there, lost in thought, until something caught his eye—a figure on the bridge above.

At first, he couldn't quite make out what was happening, but then it became clear: a woman was falling. Her body tumbled through the air, hitting the water with a splash that broke the stillness. Orsino's heart stopped.

Without a second thought, he sprinted toward the river and dove in, the cold water shocking his system as he searched for the woman. His hands moved frantically, desperate to find her, until finally, his fingers brushed against fabric. He pulled her to the surface, gasping for air as he held her in his arms, carrying her to the shore with unwavering determination.

As he laid her on the ground, his breath caught in his throat. On her finger was a ring—the same ring he had given Olly. His heart pounded as he turned her face toward him, and the shock nearly made him collapse.

It was Seraphina.

The face he hadn't seen since he was a child was now before him, older but unmistakable. His sister. The one he thought he had lost forever. "Seraphina," he whispered, his voice trembling.

He carried her to his car, his mind a whirlwind of emotions—shock, relief, confusion. He drove as fast as he could to his family home, dialing his father, Magnus, on the way. "Dad," he said, his voice urgent, "call the family doctor. It's Seraphina. I found her. I'll be there soon."

Magnus was stunned. "Seraphina? Are you sure? How—"

"Just call the doctor!" Orsino interrupted, his voice breaking.

When Orsino arrived home, Magnus was waiting at the door. As soon as he saw his daughter, he froze. Tears welled up in his eyes as he took her from Orsino's arms. "My baby," he sobbed, kissing her forehead. "Where were you? I thought I'd lost you forever."

But Seraphina was unconscious, her face pale and still. The family doctor arrived moments later, his face grave as he began his examination. He worked quickly, his movements precise, but the tension in the room was palpable. After what felt like an eternity, he turned to face Orsino and Magnus, his expression grim.

"I need you both to sit down," the doctor said, his tone gentle but firm.

Magnus shook his head, his voice breaking. "Just tell me. What's wrong with her?"

The doctor sighed deeply, removing his glasses. "Seraphina has severe internal bleeding in her brain. The fall caused significant trauma. While her body is unresponsive, there's a strong possibility she can hear everything around her. She can feel your presence, your words. But..."

Magnus leaned forward, gripping the edge of the bed. "But what?"

The doctor hesitated. "She's in a coma, and it's unlikely she'll regain full consciousness. Even if she does, her chances of recovery are slim. I'm so sorry."

The room fell silent. Magnus buried his face in his hands, his body shaking with silent sobs. Orsino clenched his fists, his jaw tightening as he fought back tears. "She's alive," he said firmly. "That's enough. She's alive, and we'll be here for her, no matter what."

The doctor placed a reassuring hand on Magnus's shoulder. "Speak to her. Let her know she's not alone. It can make a difference."

With that, the doctor left, giving them the space to process the devastating news.

Magnus wiped his tears and sat back beside Seraphina, gently holding her hand. He stroked it softly, his gaze lingering on her peaceful face. As his eyes moved to her fingers, something caught his attention, and he froze. A ring gleamed softly on her hand—a ring he recognized immediately.

"This... this is the ring I made," Magnus whispered, his voice filled with shock. His fingers trembled as he touched it. Turning to Orsino, he asked, "Did you put this on her hand?"

Orsino frowned, his brow furrowing. "No," he replied. "I don't know how it got there."

Magnus stared at the ring in disbelief, his voice barely a whisper. "This is one of the three rings I crafted with my own hands," he said, turning it over gently as if it held the weight of countless memories. "I gave them to you, Orsino."

Orsino nodded, his expression a mix of confusion and unease. "Yeah, I carried it with me all the time," he began, his voice tinged with hesitation. "But earlier today, I gave it to Olly... and now, I don't know how it ended up in her hands."

The truth, though unknown to them, was simple yet profound. When Olly had left the box on the bridge, Seraphina had come across it. Drawn to the rings, she had slipped one onto her finger without understanding its significance. That act had unknowingly tied her to Orsino and Magnus in a way none of them could yet comprehend.

Magnus and Orsino exchanged a look, both overwhelmed by the inexplicable connection.

"This ring," Magnus said softly, his voice trembling with emotion. "It's a sign. It's as if it led her back to us, as if fate was working to bring her home."

Orsino nodded, though his heart was heavy with questions. They couldn't ignore the gnawing curiosity that lingered—why had she fallen from the bridge into the river?

What had driven her to such a moment of despair? And another question loomed large in their minds: How had she been living all these years? Who had saved her after she disappeared?

The thought sent a shiver through Magnus as he stared at his daughter's fragile frame. "What has she been through? Where was she all this time? How did she survive?" he whispered, his voice breaking.

Orsino placed a steady hand on Magnus's shoulder. "We'll find out, Dad," he said firmly. "We'll uncover everything. But right now, what matters is that she's here, with us. She's alive."

Magnus looked at her pale face, his resolve hardening. "We'll protect her, no matter what. Whatever she's been through, she's not alone anymore."

Orsino nodded, his voice steady. "We'll make sure she knows she's safe—with us, with her family. We won't let anything hurt her again."

Still, both men couldn't deny the lingering questions in their hearts. They decided to wait for her to wake up and tell them everything herself. They knew the truth of her disappearance and the secrets of her survival were locked within her, waiting to be revealed.

Magnus sighed deeply, brushing a hand over her forehead. "When she wakes up, we'll hear her story. We'll wait as long as it takes."

Orsino nodded, a flicker of hope in his eyes. "She'll tell us everything. Until then, we'll be here for her, every step of the way."

In that moment, the room, heavy with unanswered questions and heartbreak, was filled with an unspoken promise: they would fight for Seraphina, protect her, and uncover the truth when she was ready to share it.

18

Seraphina remained still, locked in the silence of her own body. Though her eyes refused to open, her heart and mind were awake. Every day, Magnus and Orsino visited her bedside, speaking softly, recounting the days they had missed, the memories they wished to create, and the hope that lingered in their hearts. Their words wrapped around her like a fragile embrace, each syllable carrying their pain, love, and longing. Seraphina heard every word, every plea, and every confession of love, but her body betrayed her. She could not respond. She could only listen, tears threatening to form in her mind but unable to escape her still eyes.

Months passed, each one heavier than the last. The doctors worked tirelessly, adjusting medications and trying every treatment they could. One day, the lead doctor approached Orsino. "There is a new medication," the doctor explained, "but it's only available at the main hospital. Can you go and collect it?" Orsino nodded, determination shining through his worry. He would do anything to bring Seraphina back. Then, he went to the hospital.

BACK TO THE HOSPITAL: IN THE PRESENT, ORSINO'S WORLD SHATTERS IN AN UNIMAGINABLE TWIST

As Orsino lay on the bed, his eyes remained fixed on the baby, who was placed on a nearby bed. The child smiled at him, and Orsino smiled back instinctively.

While blood was being drawn, Orsino asked the doctor, "What about the mother? Where is she?"

The doctor paused. "The man said her name was Olly."

Orsino bolted upright, his heart pounding. "Olly?"

"Yes," the doctor said, confused. "Why? Do you know her?"

Orsino's voice trembled as memories flooded back."She... she was the love of my life."

He remembered her laughter, the sparkle in her eyes, and the promises they made. But most of all, he remembered the pain—when she vanished without a word, leaving him with nothing but questions and an ache that never healed.

As Orsino sat there, staring at the baby, a painful thought crossed his mind. He could almost understand why Olly might have left him. What if she had fallen for another man? What if she was pregnant with another man's child? Maybe that was why she'd disappeared without saying anything—without a single word of explanation.

Suddenly, a memory surfaced, clear and painful. He remembered that day vividly—they had come to this very hospital together, a year ago. The thought hit him hard. He remembered that day she had left, the day they had gone to the hospital because she said she had a headache. What if that day, she had found out she was pregnant? And maybe, just maybe, she didn't want to tell him. Maybe it had been too much for her, and she had to leave. He wondered if there were reports from that time. He had to know.

"Doctor," Orsino asked, his voice filled with urgency, "Do you remember Olly? She came here about a year ago. Do you remember her?"

The doctor paused for a moment, looking at him with a hint of confusion. "How can I remember? So many patients come through here every day," she replied, her tone distant.

Orsino felt his heart sink, but he wasn't ready to give up just yet. He reached into his pocket and pulled out the photo of Olly, holding it out to the doctor. "Please, take a look at this. Maybe it will help you remember her."

The moment the doctor saw the picture, her face changed. Her eyes widened with shock. Orsino noticed the change immediately, his pulse quickening.

"Oh... my goodness," the doctor whispered, her voice trembling. "I do remember her now." She stared at the photo again, her hands shaking slightly. "She had come here with what she thought was just a headache, but... she was suffering from something much more serious."

Orsino's breath hitched in his throat. "What do you mean?"

The doctor's face grew grave, and she lowered her gaze, as if the weight of the memory was too much to bear. "She had a rare disease in her brain, Orsino. It was something incurable, with no medication to help her. She only had a few months... maybe a year to live." She paused, her voice faltering. "She didn't even know it herself at first. It was only when we did the tests that we found out. She was in shock, pleading with me for any kind of medicine, anything that could save her... but sadly, there was nothing we could do. I could see the fear in her eyes. She knew, deep down, that her time was running out."

Orsino's world went still. His mind raced, trying to process the doctor's words. "No... that can't be... why didn't she tell me? Why didn't she say anything?"

The doctor looked at him, sympathy in her eyes. "She probably didn't want you to know. She was trying to protect you from the pain of losing her. It's likely she left because she didn't want you to see her suffer. She must have thought it would be easier for you if she disappeared."

Orsino's heart shattered into a million pieces. He couldn't breathe. Every fiber of his being felt like it was being torn apart. Olly—his Olly—had been dying, and he had never known. All the time she had been with him, she had been fighting a battle he couldn't see. She had kept it all hidden, perhaps out of love, or maybe out of fear. And he had never known the truth.

His hands clenched into fists, his nails digging into his palms. "But why? Why didn't she tell me? Why would she leave me like that?" Orsino's voice cracked, his emotions spilling over, mixing with anger, confusion, and grief. "Why did she have to go through all that alone? Why couldn't I be there for her?"

The doctor's face softened, but there was nothing she could say to ease the pain in Orsino's heart. She looked away, giving him space to process the devastating revelation. Orsino sank back onto the bed, his thoughts spiraling into an endless abyss.

Back at the custody center, Morwen was being interrogated. The officers pressed him with questions.

"How can you claim this child as yours?" one officer asked.

Morwen's voice was strained but defiant. "Because he is mine. He's my son. Olly and I... we had a child together."

The officer's eyes narrowed. "And what proof do you have of that?"

Morwen faltered, his voice dropping. "I don't need proof. I know he's mine."

"We'll need a DNA test to confirm," the officer said firmly.

Morwen's confidence wavered, but he nodded. "Fine. Do whatever you need to."

When they arrived at the hospital for the test, the scene was surreal. Orsino was in the same room, still recovering from his earlier blood donation, and the baby lay in a crib nearby. The moment Morwen saw the child, tears streamed down his face.

"My baby," he whispered, rushing to the crib. He knelt beside it, his hands trembling as he touched the child's tiny hand. "You're here. Daddy's here."

The child stared at him, uncomprehending but calm.

The officers quickly intervened, pulling Morwen back. "Step away. We need to conduct the tests."

Orsino, watching the scene, felt an unease creeping into his chest. He approached Morwen cautiously. "Who are you to Olly? Were you two together? And how are you claiming to be the father of this child?"

Morwen's expression darkened. "Who am I? Who are you to question me about my child?"

The tension in the room was palpable. To settle the matter, the doctors decided to test both Morwen and Orsino's DNA. The wait was agonizing. Morwen paced the room, muttering under his breath, "This is absurd. He's my son. He has to be."

Orsino sat silently, his mind racing with questions. Could it be true? Could this child somehow be connected to him?

When the results finally arrived, the doctor's face was unreadable. She held two envelopes.

"Morwen," she began carefully, "you are not the father of this child."

The words hit Morwen like a physical blow. He stumbled back, shaking his head in disbelief. "No. That's not possible. That's not... how can that be?"

"And Orsino," the doctor continued, her voice softer, "you are the child's biological father."

The room seemed to freeze. Orsino's breath caught, his heart pounding. He was the father? A mix of emotions surged through him—joy, confusion, grief.

Morwen, meanwhile, crumbled. "No," he whispered, sinking to the floor. "No, no, no. This can't be. My whole life... everything... it was all a lie?"

He looked up at Orsino, his face contorted with anguish. "You asked about Olly, didn't you? You wanted to know where she is? She's dead. She died giving birth to your son."

Orsino felt the ground shift beneath him. His knees buckled, and he clutched the edge of a table for support. "She's... gone?" he murmured.

"Yes," Morwen said, his voice breaking. "And now, even this—this one thing I thought was mine—it's gone too. I have nothing. Nothing!"

Morwen began pacing, his hands clawing at his hair. "How could she do this to me? How could she lie to me? How could she leave me like this?"

The officers stepped forward. "Morwen, it's time to go. You're under arrest."

Morwen approached the crib one last time. He gazed at the child, his tears falling freely. "Goodbye, little one," he whispered. "It was nice meeting you."

He turned to Orsino, his eyes hollow. "Take care of him," he said.

Before anyone could react, Morwen grabbed a gun from one of the officers. Chaos erupted as shouts filled the room.

"I don't deserve to live," Morwen said, his voice eerily calm.

"Morwen, no!" Orsino shouted, rushing toward him.

But it was too late. Morwen raised the gun to his head and pulled the trigger. The sound was deafening, and the room was engulfed in chaos. Blood pooled on the floor as everyone stood frozen, the weight of what had just happened settling over them.

Orsino sank to the ground, holding his head in his hands. The baby let out a soft cry, breaking the silence. It was a sound of life—a fragile reminder of hope amidst the tragedy.

19

The room was filled with a mix of emotions. Orsino held his son tightly in his arms, his tears falling freely onto the baby's soft skin. His heart swelled with a mixture of love and pain. "You are my baby," he whispered, the words trembling with the weight of everything he had been through. "Your life begins now."

His son's eyes were clear—the surgery was a success. Orsino thanked the doctors for their care and effort, feeling deeply grateful.

He glanced at the small bottle in his hand—the medication for Seraphina that his home doctor had asked him to get. It was a glimmer of hope in the midst of so much uncertainty. The road ahead would be long, but as he looked down at his son, there was a brief moment of peace.

Orsino left the hospital with a glimmer of happiness. He had a son now, a little boy to care for and protect. Yet, the undeniable truth remained—. Olly. His beloved Olly—gone forever. She had given him the gift of their child, but in doing so, she had left him. Forever.

He arrived home, and the familiar sights of his childhood brought a bittersweet comfort. His father, Magnus, was sitting quietly in his room, lost in thought. Orsino walked in, his baby boy in his arms, and Magnus looked up in surprise.

"Dad," Orsino said softly, his voice thick with emotion. "You're a granddad now."

Magnus blinked, his eyes widening as he looked down at the tiny, perfect face of his grandson. The tears that filled his eyes were not just tears of joy, but of sorrow, of loss, and of love. He slowly reached out, taking the baby into his arms.

Magnus's voice trembled. "He's beautiful, Orsino. Our family... our family is finally whole again."

"Where... where's Olly?" Magnus asked, his voice barely above a whisper.

Orsino's heart clenched as he answered, the pain of the words cutting deep. "I'm sorry, Dad. She... she died while giving birth to him. And she left me a year ago. She had a rare brain disease. The doctors said she only had a few months to live. She's no more with us."

The room seemed to grow heavy with grief as Magnus wiped away the tears that had spilled down his cheeks. He was devastated for Olly, but he was also filled with a new sense of love and hope for his grandson. A new life had arrived, and with it, a chance to heal, to love, and to protect. "She was such a beautiful woman," he said, his voice filled with sadness, "I'm so sorry for your loss, my son."

Orsino's heart ached, but he knew there was no turning back. He smiled faintly, trying to hold onto the happiness he felt for his son. "But now... now we have him. And I want you to help me choose his name."

Magnus gazed down at the baby, his face softening. After a long pause, he spoke the name that seemed to fit perfectly. "Flint."

Orsino repeated the name to himself, feeling a sense of peace wash over him. "Flint," he whispered, smiling. "Flint it is."

His son had a name now. And though it was bittersweet, Orsino couldn't deny the surge of love he felt. He would protect this little boy with everything he had.

Orsino stood up, cradling Flint in his arms once more, and walked toward his sister's room. Seraphina had still not opened her eyes, her body still trapped in the coma that had haunted her for so long. But Orsino was determined to show her their new family—her new family. He walked into her room quietly, as though afraid to disturb the stillness.

"Seraphina," he said softly, bending down so she could hear him. "Look. You're an aunt now."

He gently placed Flint's small hand in hers. The warmth of the baby's skin against hers was enough to stir something deep inside Seraphina. Orsino watched in stunned silence as tears slowly welled up in her closed eyes, the first sign of life he had seen from her in months.She couldn't move, couldn't open her eyes, but somehow, her soul was speaking through the tears.

His heart pounded in his chest. "Seraphina... Seraphina, are you awake? Can you hear me?"

"Dad!" Orsino shouted, his voice filled with a mix of hope and disbelief. "Dad, come quick!"

Magnus entered the room, and his heart skipped a beat when he saw the tear on Seraphina's face. He gently wiped it away, his hand trembling. "I'm here, my love. I'm always here for you," he whispered. "No matter how old you get, you're still my baby."

Tears filled Magnus's eyes as he gazed at Seraphina, and then at Flint, the newest member of their family. "Flint will protect you," he said softly, almost as if to reassure Seraphina that even though she had been in a coma for so long, she wasn't alone. "We'll protect you."

It was a bittersweet moment, filled with love and sorrow, joy and sadness. They had all been through so much, but now, in this moment, there was a quiet hope that maybe, just maybe, things could begin to heal.

Seraphina's journey to regain her memories had been a slow and painful one. Each time she remembered something from her past, tears would fall from her eyes. She couldn't speak, but her tears spoke volumes. Her body, broken and trapped, was learning to communicate again.

And then it came—a memory that had been buried so deep within her, hidden away by the mind as if to protect her from the pain. It was the memory of the day her mother had been attacked by a wild water animal, an event so traumatic it had shaken her very existence. She could now see it vividly—the panic, the fear in her mother's eyes as the creature lunged, the chaos that followed.

She remembered falling hard onto the boat's surface during the commotion, the impact so severe it had left her unconscious. That was the moment everything changed, the moment her mind had shut down, locking away all her past memories. She had woken up after the accident, a blank slate, unable to recall anything about her life before that day.

But now, the pieces were returning, one by one, as if her mind had finally decided it was time to face what had been hidden for so long. Each fragment of her past came with a wave of emotion—grief, confusion, and an aching sense of longing for the life she had lost.

Now, as she began to regain those memories, it was as if a movie played in her mind, each scene more vivid than the last. She remembered the woman who had saved her. The one whom she had called mother, Nina.

Nina's past

Nina—her name carried the weight of a story she never asked for. She was an orphan, born into a world that gave her no family to hold on to, no shoulders to lean on. Her earliest memories were of a quiet orphanage, where the only lullaby she knew was the echo of her own sobs.

But Nina wasn't one to give in. From a young age, she displayed a sharp intellect and a rare sensitivity that made her stand out. She was brilliant in her studies, devouring books and mastering subjects with a determination that left everyone in awe. Her teachers admired her drive, and her peers envied her resilience. Nina had a fire inside her, one that burned despite the loneliness that surrounded her.

As the years passed, her brilliance became her armor. She worked tirelessly, knowing that education was her way out of the shadows. She earned scholarships, aced exams, and, eventually, graduated at the top of her class.

When Nina finally stepped into the working world, she was unstoppable. Her first job was at a prestigious company, where her talent quickly set her apart. Her ideas were innovative, her projects flawless, and her work ethic unmatched. It wasn't long before she climbed the corporate ladder, earning accolades and becoming the highest-paid employee in her company.

Each night, Nina would come home to her beautiful house, the warm glow of its lights doing little to comfort her. The walls were adorned with art, the furniture immaculate, and the rooms spacious—but they were silent.

But what did all of it mean? Nina found herself questioning everything. She lived in a beautiful house, had all the luxuries anyone could dream of, but none of it filled the aching void in her heart. Every day she returned home after another long day of work, only to sit alone at the dinner table, staring at the empty chair across from her. There was no one waiting for her, no one to share a meal with, no one to talk to about the little things—the events of her day, her worries, her thoughts. She realized then how empty her life had become.

"What is all this for?" she asked herself one night, staring out the window, watching the city lights flicker in the distance. "Money, success... What is it all worth if there's no one to share it with? What is a home, really, if there's no one in it who loves you?"

As the days turned into weeks and months, Nina's loneliness grew. No matter how much she accomplished, no matter how many projects she nailed, she couldn't shake the emptiness inside. The more she succeeded, the more disconnected she felt. She had climbed the ladder of success, but with each step, it felt like she was drifting further away from herself—further away from the life she had always imagined.

It all came crashing down one night after a long, exhausting day at work. Nina couldn't do it anymore. "I can't," she whispered to herself. She felt like she was suffocating, the walls of her house closing in around her.

"I'm tired. Tired of working for nothing, tired of living a life that feels so... empty.".

"I need to get out," she thought, grabbing her car keys.

Nina drove aimlessly, the city lights blurring into streaks of gold and white as tears filled her eyes. She didn't know where she was going—she just wanted to escape. "Life," she whispered to herself, "take me somewhere. Anywhere. I can't do this anymore."

The road eventually led her to the ocean. She parked her car and stepped out, the salty breeze hitting her face. The vast expanse of water stretched out before her, dark and infinite, its waves crashing against the shore as if calling out to her.

Without hesitation, Nina walked toward the water. There was a small boat tied to the shore, and she climbed into it, her hands trembling as she untied the rope. The boat drifted out into the ocean, carried by the gentle waves.

Nina sat down, staring out at the endless horizon. "Ocean," she whispered, her voice breaking. "Please take me. I don't want to live anymore."

She lay back, letting the rocking of the boat and the soothing sound of the waves lull her into a sense of surrender. As the stars twinkled above, her eyes grew heavy, and she drifted into a deep sleep, tears still wet on her cheeks.

Nina woke up to the sound of rain. It was early morning, and the sky was overcast, casting a gray hue over the ocean. Heavy droplets fell from the sky, soaking her clothes and hair. The once-calm ocean was now restless. Waves crashed against her small boat, rocking it violently.

She sat up, disoriented, when something caught her eye—a small boat in the distance, barely staying afloat. Squinting through the rain, Nina saw a figure—a child—lying unconscious on the sinking vessel. Her heart stopped.

"Oh my God," she gasped. "Is that a child?"

Without thinking, Nina grabbed the oars and began rowing toward the other boat. The rain lashed against her skin, and the waves fought her with every stroke, but she didn't stop.

"Hold on!" she shouted, though she knew the child couldn't hear her. "I'm coming!"

The journey felt endless, but she finally reached the sinking boat. Leaning over, she grabbed the small, lifeless body and pulled it into her boat. Her hands trembled as she looked down at the child—a little girl, her face pale, her body limp. Around the girl's neck was a delicate chain with a pendant. Nina held it up, squinting through the rain to read the name engraved on it: "Seraphina."

"Seraphina," Nina called softly, shaking the girl gently. "Can you hear me? Wake up, please."

The child didn't stir. Panic surged through Nina as she turned her boat back toward the shore. She rowed with all her strength, her arms aching, her heart pounding. The rain began to lighten as she approached land, the waves finally calming.

When she reached the shore, Nina lifted Seraphina into her arms and carried her to the car. She placed the child in the passenger seat and turned on the heater, desperate to warm her up.

Then, as if by a miracle, Seraphina's eyelids fluttered open. Her gaze met Nina's, and tears filled her wide, innocent eyes.

"Mom?" Seraphina whispered, her voice weak but filled with emotion. "Mom, where were you? I missed you. Please don't leave me."

Nina froze, her breath catching in her throat. The little girl's arms wrapped around her, holding her tightly. For the first time in her life, someone was holding her like this—needing her, calling her "Mom."

Tears streamed down Nina's face as she hugged Seraphina back, overwhelmed by emotions she couldn't put into words.

"Mom," the child said again, her voice trembling.

Nina's heart broke and healed all at once. She didn't know who this child was or where she had come from, but none of that mattered. In that moment, she knew that the ocean had given her a gift—a reason to live.

"I'll never leave you," Nina whispered, her voice shaking. "I promise, Seraphina. I'll never leave you."

Seraphina looked up at her with trust, her tear-streaked face filled with relief. "Where are we going, Mom?"

Nina smiled through her tears, her heart fuller than it had ever been. "Let's go home, Seraphina," she said softly. "Let's go home."

For the first time in her life, Nina felt whole. She had found her purpose, her family, her reason to keep going. The ocean had taken her pain and given her love—a love she never knew she needed.

20

Nina gripped the steering wheel tightly as the car sped down the quiet road. Her heart felt heavy, but not in a bad way—it was full, bursting with emotions she hadn't felt in years. Alive. That's the only word that came to her mind as she glanced at the little girl beside her. Seraphina, with her innocent eyes and curious nature, was the reason Nina had found herself again.

"I left home thinking I'd never return," Nina thought as tears welled up in her eyes. "But now I'm going back—not alone, but with love, with someone who calls me Mom."

When they reached Nina's house in Cloverfield, Seraphina looked out the window and smiled brightly. "Mom, is this where we'll live?" she asked, her voice laced with excitement and warmth. Nina nodded, holding back tears.

Seraphina stepped out of the car, her face lighting up as she looked at the house. "Mom, let's go inside," she said cheerfully, tugging on Nina's arm.

Nina opened the door, and as they walked in, memories of solitude were replaced with hope. "You take some rest," Nina said gently. "I'll make us something special to eat."

For the first time in years, Nina felt joy in the kitchen. She wasn't just cooking; she was cooking for someone. Someone who wanted her. "Someone is waiting for me.

Someone wants my food," she thought. "This is what it means to feel alive."

At the dinner table, Nina watched Seraphina savor every bite of the meal. "Mom," Seraphina exclaimed, "this is so tasty!"

Nina couldn't hold back her tears anymore. She wiped her eyes quickly and said, "Eat as much as you want, my love. I'm always here for you."

As Nina looked at Seraphina, she couldn't help but wonder about her past. "Who were her parents?" Nina thought. "Why would they leave her in the middle of the ocean like that? Did they abandon her?"

Nina made a silent vow then and there: no matter what had happened to Seraphina in the past, she would give her all the love she deserved. "I'll be her family," Nina resolved. "She doesn't need to feel the pain of being unwanted."

Years passed, and Nina and Seraphina created a life full of joy and adventure. They traveled to different places, making memories that made Nina's heart feel whole again. Every time Seraphina called her "Mom," Nina felt a happiness so deep it brought tears to her eyes.

One day, during a vacation to Silverbay, Seraphina fell in love with the place. "Mom," she said, her eyes sparkling, "why don't we move here? It's so beautiful, and I'd love to stay!"

Nina hesitated. She wanted Seraphina to be happy but also wanted her to have the best future possible. After some thought, she replied, "Sweetheart, I think it's a wonderful idea. How about you do your higher education here? Silverbay has excellent schools, and I want you to build a bright future for yourself." Nina paused for a moment, her face filled with a mix of love and concern. "But, I'll need to stay in Cloverfield for work. My company is based there, and I can't leave. So, you'll have to go on your own for now." Despite the sadness in her heart, she knew this was the best decision for Seraphina's future.

Overjoyed, Seraphina hugged Nina tightly. "Thank you, Mom! I promise I'll make you proud!"

Nina worked tirelessly to make the transition smooth. She bought an apartment for Seraphina, made sure it was close to her university, and handled all the admissions. Before Seraphina left for Silverbay, Nina handed her a small envelope filled with money.

"Keep this with you," Nina said. "Use it whenever you need it. I want you to live your life the way you want and come back to Cloverfield after achieving all your dreams."

"I will, Mom," Seraphina promised, tears in her eyes. "I'll become as successful as you and make you proud."

As Seraphina waved goodbye, Nina stood by the door, watching her daughter leave to begin a new chapter of her life. "My little girl has grown up," Nina thought, her heart swelling with pride and a hint of sadness. "I can't wait to see her succeed."

Life at work became Nina's new focus. Every day felt different now, driven by her purpose to support Seraphina. Months passed, and while Nina missed Seraphina dearly, she poured herself into her job, where she was widely admired for her intelligence and dedication.

One day, a new colleague named Lucas joined the company. "Welcome," Nina greeted him warmly during his first day.

Lucas quickly realized Nina was not just an ordinary employee. At a company event celebrating her achievements, she received multiple awards, being hailed as the smartest and highest-paid employee. Lucas was intrigued—and envious.

After the event, Lucas approached her. "You're incredible, Nina," he said. "I've never met anyone as hardworking as you."

Nina laughed softly. "It's nothing, really," she replied, brushing off the compliment.

They began talking more at work, and one day, Lucas invited her to dinner. Nina agreed, thinking it would be a casual meal between colleagues.

Over dinner, the conversation turned personal. After a few drinks, Lucas asked, "What are your future plans?"

Nina, slightly intoxicated, smiled. "To support my daughter and see her succeed in life. That's all I want."

Lucas's eyes widened. "You have a daughter?"

"Yes," Nina said, smiling. "She's studying in Silverbay. She loves it there."

"What about your husband?" Lucas asked.

Nina hesitated, her guard slipping under the influence of the alcohol. "I'm not married," she admitted. "I don't even have a boyfriend. Seraphina isn't my biological daughter. I found her years ago, abandoned in the ocean. She called me 'Mom,' and I couldn't abandon her."

Lucas listened, seemingly moved by her story. "You're an incredible person, Nina," he said, hugging her.

The next day, at work, a major project was announced in the morning meeting. The room buzzed with excitement as the team listened attentively to the details. It was a high-profile assignment, one that would showcase the company's capabilities and undoubtedly lead to a promotion for whoever handled it the best.

As the project was laid out, all eyes in the room turned to Nina. She was known for her brilliance and her ability to tackle complex tasks with ease. The promotion was practically in her hands if she succeeded. Everyone knew it, and Nina, ever humble, simply nodded in acknowledgment when the project leader mentioned her name.

But across the room, Lucas clenched his fists. His face, though calm on the outside, was filled with simmering resentment. He had worked hard to earn recognition, but it always seemed to slip from his grasp. Now, it looked like Nina was going to steal this opportunity too. She was the golden child, the one everyone respected, and it felt like there was no room for him in the spotlight.

As the meeting wrapped up, the team dispersed, but Lucas couldn't shake his thoughts. I need that promotion. I need to prove I'm just as capable as Nina. She can't just get everything handed to her.

Later that day, Lucas approached Nina at her desk, his voice casual but sharp. "So, when do you think you'll start the project? The whole team's looking forward to seeing your work," he said, trying to sound supportive but secretly hoping to get a glimpse of her process. Maybe he could find a way to outshine her after all.

Nina smiled, oblivious to the envy stirring within Lucas. "I'll start it today, should be pretty straightforward," she said, not realizing that her simple confidence was driving Lucas further into resentment.

Lucas forced a tight smile, trying to hide his frustration. "Right... of course," he replied, his tone colder than intended.

Nina gave him a polite nod. "Well, good luck with your own tasks," she said cheerfully. "I'll see you around. Bye!"

She grabbed her bag, stood up, and walked out of the office, leaving Lucas to stew in his feelings. As she disappeared out the door, he stared after her, an unsettling mix of jealousy and ambition brewing inside him.

The next morning, Nina arrived at the office as usual. She was greeted by the familiar hum of office chatter and the sound of clicking keyboards. As she walked toward her desk, she noticed Lucas sitting at his own workstation, his eyes fixed on her with a mix of anticipation and frustration.

"Good morning, Nina," he said, flashing her a smile that didn't quite reach his eyes.

"Morning, Lucas," she replied, settling into her chair and opening her computer.

Lucas lingered for a moment before speaking up again, unable to mask the impatience in his voice. "So, uh, how much have you finished on the project?"

Nina glanced at him briefly before responding nonchalantly. "Oh, I finished it last night. It was easy, honestly," she said with a shrug, the confidence in her tone clear.

Lucas blinked, taken aback by her response. He hadn't expected her to have completed it so quickly. A surge of jealousy rushed through him, but he quickly masked it with forced curiosity. "Really? Wow, that's impressive. So, when are you going to submit it?" he asked, trying to keep his tone casual.

Nina leaned back in her chair, tapping her pen on the desk as she thought for a moment. "Well, I thought of submitting it today, but then I realized that might seem a bit too fast. So, I'll submit it tomorrow during the meeting," she said with a small smile.

Lucas struggled to keep his composure. Inside, his mind was racing. She's already finished it? Why is she always one step ahead of me? The jealousy that simmered within him started to boil. He forced a smile, though it felt unnatural. "Oh, that's nice. Yeah, take your time," he said, trying to hide the bitterness in his voice.

As Nina turned back to her work, Lucas felt a growing sense of competition. He knew the project was meant for Nina, that everyone in the company expected her to excel. But it didn't sit well with him. Lucas wanted that promotion, and he wasn't about to let Nina stand in his way.

Back at Nina's home, she was winding down after a long day of work. Just as she settled into her chair with a book, she heard the doorbell ring. Surprised, she got up to answer it. When she opened the door, she was even more surprised to see Lucas standing there in the dark of the evening, holding a bouquet of flowers.

"Hey, Nina," Lucas said with a warm smile, holding out the flowers. "These are for you."

Nina blinked in surprise but smiled, accepting the bouquet. "Thank you, Lucas. Come in," she said, stepping aside to let him in.

As Lucas walked in, Nina led him to the living room. "I didn't expect to see you tonight," she remarked as she set the flowers on the coffee table.

"I thought you could use a little surprise," Lucas replied, sitting down beside her.

They talked for a while, laughing and sharing stories. Eventually, Nina showed him pictures of Seraphina, her face lighting up as she spoke about her daughter's life in Silverbay. Lucas was pretending to be interested as Nina spoke.

The conversation shifted as the evening went on, the mood between them becoming more intimate. Before long, their connection deepened, and the night took an unexpected turn. They spent a passionate and steamy night together, their previous conversations forgotten in the haze of desire.

The next morning, Nina woke up, already prepared for work. She looked over at Lucas, still asleep beside her. She gently nudged him awake. "Lucas," she whispered, "it's time to get up."

As he stirred, he smiled lazily, his voice soft. "Last night was amazing."

Nina nodded, a small smile playing on her lips. "Yeah, it really was," she replied.

Then, as she began to grab her things to leave, Lucas stopped her, holding her project file. "Why don't you let me handle this?" he asked, his tone more serious now. "It's just work to you, but it's everything to me."

Nina frowned, confused. "Lucas, you're joking, right?"

His expression hardened. "No, I'm serious. Give it to me."

Nina stepped back, shocked. "You spent the night with me for this? Lucas, how could you?"

Lucas smirked and pulled out his phone. "If you don't give me the project, I'll show everyone this video from last night. Imagine what your daughter or your colleagues would think."

Nina froze, her heart pounding. "Lucas, please. Don't do this."

"You think Seraphina is your daughter? She's not even your real child," Lucas sneered. "Face it, Nina. You're lonely and pathetic. You have nothing."

Nina felt her world shatter. Lucas had targeted her deepest fears and insecurities.

Nina froze, her world crumbling around her. "Please," she begged. "Don't do this. Don't involve my daughter."

Lucas's expression turned cold. "Give me everything—your project, your wealth—and leave. Disappear from here, or I'll ruin you."

"Fine," she whispered, her voice breaking. "I'll give you everything. Just don't harm Seraphina."

Tears streaming down her face, Nina packed her things and left, leaving behind her home, her career, and everything she had worked for. As she walked away, broken and betrayed, Lucas watched her go, his smirk fading as he closed the door behind her. In her haste to leave, Nina had forgotten to take her phone, leaving it behind as she disappeared.

Nina drove far, far away, her sobs echoing in the silence. Everything she had built was gone, and once again, she was left with nothing but pain. She couldn't bear the thought of facing Seraphina now—not after everything that had happened. She had lost everything, and she didn't have the courage to tell her daughter the truth.

And so, with no destination in mind, Nina disappeared, leaving behind only the remnants of her shattered life.

A few months later...

Lucas sat at Nina's desk, flipping through papers, when her phone buzzed. He glanced at the screen—it was a message from Seraphina.

"Mom, I'm pregnant."

Lucas smirked. He had been the one replying to Seraphina all along, pretending to be Nina. He couldn't help but feel a sense of control over the tangled mess he had created. But Seraphina thought it was her mom.

21

Seventeen years had passed, and Seraphina remained trapped in a motionless state—her body unresponsive, her eyes closed, yet her mind was painfully alert. She could feel everything around her, the steady pulse of time, and the weight of two rings resting on her hand. One was her husband's, a symbol of their love, while the other was the mysterious ring her father, Magnus, had crafted for her—a masterpiece of intricate design, imbued with hidden power. It had been designed by her father as a memory of her, because he had believed her to be dead. But that ring now served as a silent link to her past, a connection to everything she had lost, bridging her to the family she had forgotten.

The ring on her finger was the same one she had worn the day her life had been ripped apart. Its presence was a constant reminder of her father's brilliance, the love he had poured into it, and the mystery that had bound her fate to its secrets. She could feel the weight of its significance, both in her fading memories and in the silence of the years that followed.

But now, Seraphina's mind slowly unraveled the tangled threads of the past. She could remember everything—the life she had once known, her family, and the devastating moment when it had all shattered. The horrifying image of her mother being attacked by a wild water animal came rushing back. The trauma of that moment had stolen her memories, wiping everything away in an instant. For years, Seraphina had no recollection of her past—no memory of her family or who she had been. But now, as clarity returned, she began to understand.

For years, Seraphina had no recollection of who she was, where she came from, or who had once been by her side. But after the incident, when she had fallen unconscious, a woman—an unfamiliar stranger—saved her life. As soon as Seraphina regained consciousness, disoriented and fragile, she instinctively called out to the woman, "Mom." It was as if her mind, in an attempt to protect her from the trauma, had found a way to fill the void of confusion and loss by assigning the woman a new, comforting role in her life.

The woman, whose name was Nina, had cared for Seraphina, nurtured her, and loved her as though Seraphina were her own daughter. And so, Seraphina had clung to that new bond, believing, in that moment, that Nina was the only family she had left, the only one who could make her feel whole again.

It all rushed back to her now, the clarity she had been missing for so long. She had fallen in love with a guy named Darwen and had kids with him. She remembered the vacation to Mistwood with her family—how she had been pushed off a bridge by Morwen. The impact with the rocks had left her unconscious, and it was only by Orsino's intervention that she had been saved. He had rescued her, bringing her to safety, but it had been 17 years since then. During all that time, she had been trapped in a motionless state—unable to wake, speak, or even open her eyes.

As she lay in this coma, Seraphina's memories slowly returned. She realized the painful truth: she had lost her past and, with it, the knowledge of her true family. She had never known Orsino, her brother, or Magnus, her father. They had existed in her past, but she had no memory of them—no memory of the love and life she had shared with them.

Her husband and children had likely thought she was dead, unaware that she was still alive, trapped in this silent world. All Seraphina wanted was to see them again, to be reunited with her family, to feel their love once more. But she couldn't. She couldn't speak, couldn't move, couldn't reach out to her father to ask him to bring her back to her family.

The weight of this overwhelming pain was unbearable. She longed to meet the woman who had cared for her, the one she had mistakenly called "Mom" all these years. She wanted to thank her for her kindness, even though she now understood the truth.

Seventeen years had passed, and she was still here, unable to escape the prison of her own body. All Seraphina wanted was to tell her family the truth—to tell them she was alive—and to feel their arms around her once more. But for now, all she could do was wait—wait for the day she could finally wake up, move, and speak to the ones she loved.

22

Present Day

As Darwen was driving to meet his son, Ethan, after receiving a call from him about Catherine's disappearance, his mind raced with questions. He parked his car outside Catherine's apartment, where Ethan was anxiously waiting for him.

Darwen stepped out and asked, "When was the last time you saw her?"

Ethan replied, "The last time I saw her was at Dana's birthday party. After that, she said she had an evening tuition class, and then... I don't know. She hasn't been back since."

Darwen frowned, trying to make sense of the situation. "Let's check the apartment's CCTV footage."

They accessed the footage, which revealed that Catherine had left her apartment on Sunday evening. Darwen turned to Ethan and asked, "Where do you think she might have gone?"

Ethan hesitated before saying, "Usually, she doesn't go anywhere on Sundays. She stays in."

Darwen pressed him, "Think, Ethan. Is there a place she could have gone? A friend's house? Somewhere familiar?"

Ethan suddenly remembered. "Oh! Dana's park! She might be there. Maybe she went there."

Without wasting any time, they drove to Dana's park. When they arrived, they noticed workers busy cleaning the pool and sanitizing the surrounding area. Darwen and Ethan approached one of the workers and asked to see the CCTV footage of the park.

The worker shook his head. "Sorry, we can't let you see it. It's against protocol."

Darwen's instincts screamed that something was wrong. He stepped closer, glaring at the worker. "You're hiding something," he said coldly. When the worker refused again, Darwen lost his patience. A heated argument turned into a scuffle, and Darwen punched the worker, forcing him to hand over access to the CCTV footage.

Ethan and Darwen watched the footage intently. The video showed Catherine arriving at the park and approaching the pool. Moments later, Dana appeared. They talked briefly, and then, shockingly, Dana pushed Catherine into the pool. After a few minutes, Catherine didn't resurface. Instead, Dana jumped in, and when she emerged, she was alone.

Darwen's breath caught as the footage ended. "Where is Catherine?" he muttered, fury and fear etched on his face.

Ethan suddenly remembered something Dana had once mentioned. "Dad! Dana always said she had a secret bunker inside her pool. What if Catherine is there?"

Darwen's face paled at the thought. Together, they rushed to the pool. The workers had drained the water during their cleaning, leaving the pool empty. Inside the deep end of the pool, they spotted an entrance—a concealed passage leading to a door.

Darwen and Ethan hurried through the passage. They pushed open the door, and what they saw inside made Darwen's knees buckle. His heart felt like it had stopped, and his mind struggled to comprehend the scene before him.

Inside the bunker, the dim light revealed something they could never have imagined.

Inside the bunker, Seraphina sat, her presence shattering the reality Darwen and Ethan had clung to for years. The woman they thought was gone forever—dead—was right there before them. Darwen's voice trembled as he fell to his knees. "Seraphina... Seraphina..."

She turned at the sound of her name, her face lighting up despite the exhaustion etched into her features. Tears streamed down her cheeks as she screamed out in pain, not just physical but the pain of years lost. Without hesitation, she threw herself into Darwen's arms. Both of them knelt there, embracing tightly, as if holding on could undo the years of separation.

"Darwen, my love," Seraphina whispered through sobs. "I missed you so much. I thought... I thought I would never move again, never see you again." Her voice cracked with the weight of her emotions. Then she turned, her tearful eyes landing on Ethan.

Ethan, equally overwhelmed, stammered, "Mom... Mom?" His voice broke as he fell to his knees, wrapping his arms around her. "Where were you all these years? How... How are you here?"

Seraphina hugged them both, trembling with relief. "I don't know how I got here. I don't know... But before I came here, I was in a coma. For 17 years, I couldn't talk, move, or even open my eyes. It was because of that incident... I was saved. Saved by my brother."

Darwen's brow furrowed, and he pulled back slightly, looking at her in disbelief. "Brother? Seraphina, you have a brother?"

She nodded, tears still streaming down her face. "Yes, Darwen. I didn't know it myself at first. His name is Orsino. He's the one who saved me. And my father, Magnus... He looked after me."

She took a deep, steadying breath and began explaining everything—how she had lost all her past memories during their family vacation when her mother was attacked by a wild water animal. The trauma had wiped her mind clean. She was found and rescued by a woman named Nina, who became like a mother to her. For years, Seraphina lived with Nina, believing she was her only family.

"When I was in that coma for 17 years," Seraphina continued, "I started remembering everything. All the memories I had lost came back to me. I realized who I was, who my family were, and the love we shared. And yet, I don't know how I ended up here. But I'm finally awake, able to move, to talk, and to see you both again."

She hugged them tightly, her words full of love and gratitude. "I love you both so much."

As they held each other, Seraphina suddenly noticed the ring on her finger—the ring her father, Magnus, had carved. Her eyes widened as the ring began to fade, disappearing slowly before their eyes. She gasped, holding up her hand. "Look! The ring... It's disappearing. I think... I think this ring brought me here."

Darwen stared in disbelief, his emotions overwhelming him. He pulled her into his arms again, kissing her forehead, her cheeks, and finally her lips. Tears streamed down his face as he whispered, "My love... Seraphina, please don't leave me again. I love you. I've always loved you."

Seraphina cried as well, holding onto him tightly. Ethan watched his parents, his heart swelling with happiness and awe. For the first time in years, he saw his family whole again, and it struck him just how deeply his parents must have loved each other.

But then Seraphina pulled back slightly, her expression shifting to one of concern. "Where... Where is Catherine?" she asked, looking between Darwen and Ethan.

Darwen and Ethan exchanged uneasy glances before Ethan replied, "Catherine was supposed to be here. We saw on the CCTV footage that she was here... That's why we came looking. But she's nowhere to be found."

Seraphina's eyes widened as realization dawned on her. "Oh... Oh my god," she gasped. "I know where Catherine is."

Darwen and Ethan leaned in, desperate for answers. "Where?" Darwen asked urgently.

Seraphina's voice was steady but filled with urgency. "I think... we teleported. If Catherine and I switched places, then she must be where I was. She's at my father's place, in Mistwood."

Darwen and Ethan exchanged a stunned glance, but Seraphina's certainty gave them hope. Without wasting another second, they began planning their next steps, determined to find Catherine and reunite their family completely.

Catherine's Awakening in Mistwood

Catherine stirred awake, the sterile smell of medicine and the sight of a grand, unfamiliar room filling her senses. She glanced around, her eyes landing on a nurse standing nearby. "Excuse me, ma'am," Catherine called weakly.

The nurse froze, her eyes wide with disbelief. Without saying a word, she screamed and bolted out of the room, leaving Catherine stunned. "What on earth..." she muttered, confusion swirling in her mind.

Moments later, an older man entered the room. His presence was commanding, yet his expression was a mix of shock and confusion. Catherine looked at him cautiously. "Who are you? Where am I?"

Magnus stepped closer, his voice trembling. "Where is my daughter, Seraphina? How did you come here?"

Catherine frowned, trying to piece everything together. "I don't know how I got here. All I remember is that bitch Dana pushing me into the pool. That's it."

Magnus's eyes narrowed as he noticed the ring on her finger. His face paled, and he stumbled back, calling out, "Orsino! Come here, now!"

Orsino hurried into the room, his eyes widening at the sight of Catherine. His gaze quickly fell to the ring on her finger—one of the three his father had carved. "Who... Who is she?" he asked Magnus, his voice uncertain.

Magnus turned to Catherine, his voice urgent. "Do you know who the person in that picture is?" He held up a photograph of Seraphina from her youth.

Catherine nodded firmly. "Yes. She's my mom."

Both men froze, struggling to process her words. Magnus stepped closer, his hand trembling as he reached for hers. "So... you're Seraphina's child?"

"Yes," Catherine replied, now equally shocked. "Are you her father?"

Magnus's voice broke as he said, "Yes, I am her father. And this is her brother, Orsino."

Tears filled Catherine's eyes as the realization hit her. "So you're my grandfather?" she asked, her voice cracking.

Magnus nodded, his expression filled with emotion. Catherine's mind raced as she asked, "Is my mom alive?

Where is she?"

Magnus sighed deeply, the weight of years of pain evident in his voice. "Catherine... we thought she was dead. When Seraphina was a child, we went on a family vacation. It was supposed to be a happy time, but tragedy struck. During a storm, Seraphina and her mother got separated from us near the ocean.

He paused, his voice faltering as he fought back tears. "Her mother... she was swallowed by a wild water animal in the ocean. We couldn't save her. And as for Seraphina... we couldn't find her. She was just gone. For years, I believed I had lost her forever."

Magnus's voice broke, and he looked down, his hands trembling. "The guilt, the grief—it consumed me. We lost two of the most important people in our lives that day."

He paused, his eyes glistening with unshed tears. "But then Orsino found her years later in a river. She was alive, but..." Magnus hesitated, struggling to continue.

"But what?" Catherine asked urgently.

Magnus took a shaky breath. "She had been in a coma ever since. She never woke up. For all these years, she's been lying in a bed, lifeless but alive. And now, instead of her being on this bed, you're here. Catherine, how is this possible? Where is Seraphina?"

Catherine's heart pounded as she tried to make sense of it all. "I don't know," she whispered, her voice trembling. "If she's not here... then where is she?"

Catherine's mind raced as the pieces started to fall into place. Her eyes widened with sudden realization. "Wait..." she said, her voice shaky but determined. "If I'm here... where my mom was supposed to be, then... I guess she might be there too."

A sudden spark of understanding crossed her face, and she added, "Yeah... I guess we teleported."

Magnus looked at her, his expression a mixture of confusion and disbelief. "Teleported?"

Catherine placed a comforting hand on his arm. "Wait, let me call my dad." She quickly dialed Darwen's number.

Darwen answered almost immediately, his voice filled with relief. "Catherine! Where are you? Are you safe?"

"Dad," Catherine said, her voice shaking. "I'm safe. I'm at... my grandfather's home. Is Mom there with you? Please tell me she's safe too."

Before Darwen could respond, Seraphina grabbed the phone from him. "Catherine! Baby! Where are you? Are you okay?"

"Mom!" Catherine cried, tears streaming down her face. "Yes, I'm okay. I'm safe. But I need to see you. Please come."

Seraphina's voice softened, filled with love and relief. "We'll come, baby. Just stay where you are. We'll come to you."

Catherine handed the phone to Magnus, whose hands trembled as he heard his daughter's voice for the first time in years. "Seraphina?" he whispered, his voice breaking. "My baby... You can speak. You're healed."

"Yes, Dad," Seraphina replied, her voice warm and soothing. "Thanks to you. It was the rings you made—they brought us back together. They served their purpose."

Magnus's mind reeled at her words, but he couldn't deny the truth. "The rings..." he whispered, overwhelmed.

Seraphina continued, "We're all coming to Mistwood. Just wait for us."

23

The Reunion in Mistwood

When Darwen, Seraphina, and Ethan arrived at Mistwood, it was a moment of pure emotion. Seraphina ran into Magnus's arms, and they embraced tightly, both crying uncontrollably. Ethan and Catherine hugged as well, their family finally beginning to feel whole again.

Over the next few hours, Seraphina explained everything—her coma, her rescue by Magnus and Orsino, the memories she regained, and the miraculous events that had brought them all together.

As the family sat together, Catherine suddenly noticed something unusual. The ring on her finger began to fade. "Look!" she exclaimed, holding up her hand.

Everyone watched in awe as the ring disappeared entirely. Magnus nodded solemnly. "The rings... They've done what they were meant to do."

For a moment, the family sat in stunned silence. Then, laughter erupted, lightening the air. They couldn't help but marvel at the twists of fate that had brought them back together.

In that moment, they realized that no matter how fragmented their past had been, they were now a complete, happy family again.

After the heartfelt reunion at Mistwood, Seraphina's mind suddenly flashed with a memory—the woman she had always considered her mother, the one who had saved her, who had been there for her when she needed someone most. She turned to her family, her voice filled with determination. "We need to go meet her. She is my mom."

Without hesitation, the family piled into the car, driven by the urgency in Seraphina's voice. They made their way to Cloverfield, the place Seraphina once called home. But when they arrived, what they saw shocked them.

The house was no more. The structure that once held so many memories was demolished, nothing left but ruins. Seraphina's heart sank as she stared at the empty lot.

Magnus, his voice calm but filled with concern, asked, "Are you sure this is the right place?"

Seraphina nodded slowly, her eyes scanning the devastation. "I'm sure. This was home. But something's telling me... we need to go to the ocean. That's where she saved me."

They drove to the nearby ocean, Seraphina's instincts guiding them as they parked and got out of the car. The salty breeze and crashing waves seemed to beckon Seraphina forward. She ran ahead, her heart pounding in her chest.

And then, she saw it—the old car, Nina's car, sitting by the shoreline.

There, by the water, an elderly woman sat, gazing out at the vast ocean. Her posture was peaceful, as if waiting for something—or someone.

Seraphina's heart skipped a beat as she called out, "Mom! Mom! I'm here, Mom!"

Nina turned slowly, her eyes widening in disbelief. She immediately stood and ran toward Seraphina, tears streaming down her face.

The two women embraced, a moment of pure joy and love, as Seraphina's family watched from a distance, their eyes filled with emotion.

Seraphina pulled away slightly and whispered, "I'm back, Mom."

Nina, her voice trembling, replied, "I'm so sorry, my dear. I couldn't be there for you. But I knew you would come to me someday. I knew I'd see you again. My baby, I love you."

Magnus stepped forward, his eyes glistening with tears. He fell to his knees in front of Nina, his gratitude overwhelming him. "Thank you, Nina. Thank you for saving my daughter. For bringing her back to me."

Seraphina, still in Nina's arms, began to tell her everything—about the years she had lost, the coma, the rings, and how she had finally found her family again. Nina listened intently, her face a mixture of sadness and relief.

Then, Nina shared her own story—how she had found Seraphina, cared for her, and loved her as her own. She explained how she had ended up in this difficult situation, revealing that her colleague had blackmailed her, taking everything she had. But Nina had waited for this day, hoping for the chance to set things right and reunite Seraphina with her true family.

Then Seraphina took Nina's hand, her voice soft but filled with warmth. "Mom, let's go. It's time."

Nina looked at her, confused. "Where?"

Seraphina smiled, a tear slipping down her cheek. "Let's go home. I'll cook you something delicious, something I've wanted to do for so long."

The words struck Nina deep in her heart. It was the same thing she had said to Seraphina when they first met, and now, the roles had reversed. She couldn't hold back her tears, the weight of the moment overwhelming her.

They all returned to Mistwood, where Seraphina's home had become a place of healing and joy. The house was filled with laughter as everyone sat down to eat together.

Nina, still emotional, looked around at her newfound family, a smile on her face through her tears. "No matter what happens, if you have your loved ones, then living this life for just one day is enough. And I'm so thankful to have all of you here with me."

Seraphina, her voice filled with love and certainty, responded, "Mom, this is your family now. We're your family."

And for the first time in years, Nina felt truly at home. Surrounded by the people she loved, and the family that had come together despite all odds, she knew that no matter what the future held, they would face it together. They were whole.

From that day on, they lived as one, united by love and the healing of shared moments. The house, once a place of emptiness, was now filled with warmth, laughter, and the quiet comfort of being together. Their past struggles, though still present in their memories, no longer defined them. Instead, they built something new—something strong and unbreakable.

In each other, they found peace, joy, and a love that had withstood the test of time and pain. And as they sat together, they knew one thing for sure—this was where they were meant to be. Together.

"In the end, the journey is never about where you've been, but who you've become along the way."

THE END

Thank you for reading this journey. This story has been a reflection of the unpredictability of life, the resilience of the human spirit, and the enduring power of love, loss, and hope.

Through every twist, every challenge, and every revelation, the message remains clear: no matter how difficult the road, the strength to overcome is found in the heart's deepest desire to heal and move forward.

I hope this tale has inspired you to reflect on your own strength and resilience, to never stop seeking answers, and to always believe in the possibility of a better tomorrow.

This is not just a story of survival, but of transformation and connection, showing us that even in the darkest times, light can emerge.

Thank you for being a part of this journey.

With deepest gratitude,

DIVYA DISM

9 798889 632112 5